Traveling On
into
the
Light

A Melanie Kroupa Book

Traveling On into the Light ++++++

and other stories

by Martha Brooks

Orchard Books   *New York*

The author gratefully acknowledges the assistance of the Canada Council and the Manitoba Arts Council. Once again, thanks to Melanie, Shelley, Maureen, and Kirsten.

"You've Always Been Such a Good Friend to Me" appeared in a slightly different form as "The Best Weekend of My Life" in the collection *Unexpected Fictions: New Icelandic Canadian Writing*, edited by Kristjana Gunnars. Winnipeg, Canada: Turnstone Press, 1989.

Permission to quote from the following works is gratefully acknowledged. The epigraph, page vii: "Excerpts," from *Two Suns Rising* by Johnathan Star, translation copyright © 1991 by Johnathan Star. Used by permission of Bantam Books, a division of Bantam Doubleday Dell Publishing Group, Inc. In "The Kindness of Strangers" on page 17: *A Streetcar Named Desire* by Tennessee Williams. Used by permission of New Directions Publishing Corporation. In "Where Has Romance Gone?" on page 31: "Black Coffee" by Sonny Burke and Paul Francis Webster, © 1948 (renewed) Sondot Music Corporation and Webster Music Co. Used with permission. In "Where Has Romance Gone?" on page 37: "The Nearness of You." Words: Ned Washington. Music: Hoagy Carmichael. Copyright © 1937 and 1940 by Famous Music Corporation. Copyright renewed 1964 and 1967 by Famous Music Corporation. In "All the Stars in the Universe" on page 134: "Louise" by Leo Robin and Richard A. Whiting. Copyright © 1929 by Famous Music Corporation. Copyright renewed 1956 by Famous Music Corporation.

Orchard Books
95 Madison Avenue
New York, NY 10016

Manufactured in the United States of America
Book design by Chris Hammill Paul
10 9 8 7 6 5 4 3 2
The text of this book is set in 12 point Goudy Old Style.

Library of Congress Cataloging-in-Publication Data

Brooks, Martha, date.
Traveling on into the light and other stories / by Martha Brooks.
p. cm.
"A Melanie Kroupa book"—Half t.p.
Summary: A collection of short stories which focus on the difficult journeys teens take on their way to adulthood.
ISBN 0-531-06863-3. — ISBN 0-531-08713-1 (lib. bdg.)
1. Short stories, Canadian. [1. Short stories.] I. Title.
PZ7.B7975Tr 1994
[Fic]—dc20   94-9136

-†- -†- -†- -†- For Alice

Coming and going,

    life and death.

A thousand villages,

    a million houses.

Don't you get the point?

Moon in the water,

    blossom in the sky.

—Gizan

✢ ✢ ✢ ✢ Contents

The Tiniest Guitar in the World ⚔ ⚔ ⚔ ⚔

I am following Fletcher P. (Flint) Eastwood down the hall. I've been ordered to his office, where we will sit and the lid on his good eye will jump up and down like a butterfly in a frenzy before he'll calmly ask, "What's up, Petrie?"

I will respond politely, "Nothing, *sir*," because my father went to an army academy and he taught me that this always makes a good impression. It also drives Mr. Eastwood crazy. The way I say *sir*, he can't find any fault with.

He's built like a retired football player and sort of bounces when he walks. His suits—all three of them— fit too tight in the jacket and too loose in the pants. There's a little ring of blondish gray hair that sits on his ears like a costume store bald wig, and the skin on top is firebrick red. Which is why we call him Flint.

His dinky office smells of eraser crumbs and old coffee and unidentifiable aftershave. You might say it's like a second home to me.

We get inside. He closes the door. "Sit," he says to the orange chair in front of his desk.

I sit down and kick at a paper ball near my feet. Beside it is a paper clip. I pick that up so I'll have something to fiddle with.

Flint settles in behind the desk, sighs, wipes his face with a wrinkly hand. I shoot a look at him in time to catch the butterfly-in-a-frenzy eyelid maneuver. His chair makes that old familiar squeak as he leans dangerously far back. He pauses, then comes forward fast. His elbows hit the desktop with a hollow sound like distant drums.

"What's up, Petrie?"

I've twisted the paper clip so that it's like a square with half the top missing. "Nothing, *sir*."

"Goddamn it, Donald—don't patronize me. Mrs. Lindblad *saw* you outside at noon."

"What? Sir?"

"You and your friends. Robert Isles and that . . . Goran fellow—Chris. Loose brown cigarette papers. Does that ring a bell?"

Loose *brown* cigarette papers?

He leans in on me. "Are you boys selling drugs?"

The paper clip now resembles a mutilated snake.

"Put that thing down and answer me."

I toss the clip. It bounces off the desk leg and veers back, tangling itself into the laces of my boot. "No, sir," I mumble, pulling it off.

The worst thing about somebody making up their mind that you're a liar is that you can tell the truth until you're blue in the face, but they aren't going to believe you, anyway.

"What's that? What did you say?" He's practically lying on his desk.

"I said, no, sir."

"Dammit, look at me when you answer."

I look. The other eye is glass. The color doesn't quite match his good eye.

"No . . . sir."

"You know, Donald, I can't think of a single other person in this school who spends more time in this office, but it never seems to faze you."

He talks to me a lot about stuff not fazing me—my poor grades, my total disregard for the school's dress code, and my being a disturbing influence.

"You were *seen*, Donald. Outside, at *noon*. *Rolling marijuana cigarettes and selling them to the seventh-grade boys!*"

At noon. Outside at noon. Robert Isles, Chris Goran, and I found a dead squirrel. It was flattened—fairly fresh roadkill. Its mouth was open, its teeth bared. Its right arm stretched up past its ear. The other hung down around its belly. Goran starts joking around that it's lip synching. Isles is sucking on a can of root beer. Goran holds up the squirrel. Makes its left paw twitch frantically up and down. Isles spews root beer all over the ground. And that's when I get this unusual idea.

Goran's little brother, Paul, walks by with Simon Wiebe. We make them go into their classroom and bring out a pair of scissors. And what happens next is pretty amazing. Everybody hangs around watching. It's about the most creative thing I've done since I was a little kid.

"Donald, I've given you more warnings and second chances than just about anyone in the history of this school," Flint says, fishing around his shirt pocket under his gray pinstriped suit jacket. He pulls out a fresh pack of gum. "What is it you care about?" He picks at the outside wrapper. "I'd really like to know." He can't get the tab undone. He finally mangles it open and offers me a stick.

"No, thanks, sir. It's bad for my teeth."

Patiently smiling, he takes a piece of gum for himself. He's going to act all buddy-buddy now. This is the ace up his sleeve, as they say. Sometimes you go to see the vice-principal or a counselor or whatever because you really need help. I don't know if they think you *enjoy* asking for help, or what. But you're depressed. They offer you a piece of gum. You tell them your problems because who else have you got to turn to—your mother? Then they offer you some turd piece of advice that messes you up even more because on top of everything else, you now have to worry about this new evidence they have on you, and about how they'll use it against you whenever they're in the right mood and you're in the wrong place.

So much for the buddy system.

Flint leans his arm on the desk, his chin on the palm of his hairy hand. It's his I'm-open-to-anything-you-have-to-tell-me-because-I'm-a-reasonable-caring-human-being position.

"Have you given any further thought to what you might do after you leave school?"

He's leading up to my becoming a drug dealer. Or to washing dishes at Mr. Steak for the rest of my life.

"Well, sir, lately I've been thinking seriously about marine biology."

"I see." He chews away. Waits for me to continue. We've been over this ground before.

"I worry about oil spills. Stuff like that."

"Stuff . . . like . . . that," he repeats, drawing out my words like my life is some kind of free-for-all display. He wisely nods. Puckers his lips. Sniffs. I know what he's going to say next and that it will make him very very happy to say it.

"You are aware, of course, that you'll have to finish high school first. With good grades. Just when were you planning to get those?"

I feel a little nauseated. A little hot. A bit enraged. "To *get* them, sir?" I say innocently.

He slams down his hand, flat, on the desktop. I must jump about ten feet.

"Don't be smart with me! I've given you *hours* of my time. I've tried to reach you. I've been lenient with you. I've done everything I could to be the best possible friend I can. And I *am* your friend, Donald. But today just takes the cake. What are we going to do about it?"

"We?"

"Don't you know I could have you arrested right now? For trafficking? Don't you know that?"

"I wasn't selling drugs. And there's no such thing as

brown cigarette papers. Name one time you have *ever* seen a brown cigarette paper, sir."

"Well. She was obviously wrong about the color," he says, like he's thinking for the first time since I walked in here that he might be losing ground.

"She didn't see brown cigarette papers today," I say in a soft, respectful tone. "What she saw was a brown root beer can being cut up and rolled."

I sit back and wait to see what he'll do next. His face shows a real struggle. He's madly trying to stuff back whoever it is behind the vice-principal mask he dons every morning as he's getting that fat knot into his silk tie.

"A root beer can?"

"Would I make up such a thing?"

"Possibly. This may sound like a dumb question, Donald, but why would you be cutting up a root beer can?"

I take a deep breath. Might as well tell the truth. Who knows? He just might believe it.

"I was making an electric guitar, sir."

"Go on." He's got this steady bead on me, like if I blow this one I'm a dead man.

"A very small electric guitar. Not a real one, you understand, but something that looked like one. For a dead squirrel, sir. I made it so it would look as if he was really playing it. Sort of caught forever in the moment, if you know what I mean—kind of like a statue."

Flint crinkles up his forehead and allows this to register. He takes his pencil and sort of dances it between his hands. He then plops it into a stained white mug along with the other yellow pencils and cheap blue pens.

"Where is this squirrel?"

"He's lying on his back, sir, out in the school yard. I can show you if you like."

"And the guitar?"

"It's here in my pocket. I didn't have time to set him up yet, so to speak." The cold aluminum warms quickly in my fingers. "I actually didn't know if I felt like just leaving it out there, either. The guitar, I mean." I hold it out to Flint.

He takes it and studies it for a minute. Then he sort of sags over his desk.

"This actually resembles a guitar," he says, looking up at me with wonder on his face.

"Yes. I know it does," I say, suddenly very happy. It's only at this exact moment that I realize that it does. And that it's actually beautiful to look at. I start to laugh. My eyes smart.

"No. I mean truly it does," he says, pointing to the delicate strings. "How did you do those?"

"I cut the can up really fine there. I mean at that point of making it."

"You must have a *very* steady hand. This stuff looks almost *shaved.*"

"Well, I did sort of shave it. It was a kind of experimental shear-and-shave sort of thing."

"Does it actually fit the squirrel?"

"Yes, it does. We tried it out. It looks very lifelike."

"Believe me," he says, still looking at the guitar, "I know more than you think I do about what you're going through. You have an original turn of mind, Donald. If you could only find a way of using that to your benefit, instead of always using it like a suit of armor, then you'd have a sweet life."

"A sweet life?"

"Yes."

I wait for him to elaborate on this. He doesn't. He hands back my guitar. He plays with a pile of papers on his desk. "I pulled you out of your last class," he says, finally. "You might as well go on home now."

"Really? Thanks."

Flint's biggest problem is that he still likes kids, but we've finally worn him out.

I pause at the door, and on a kind of whim I say, "You really should be looking into another line of work, Mr. Eastwood. Something that makes you feel happier."

"That would be terrific, Don," he says tiredly. "If I could only find the energy."

"You'll figure something out," I say.

I close the door as soft as a feather, so as not to jar his nerves any further.

I start down the hall. This is a small private school. I've been coming here ever since three quarters of the way through first grade. The elementary school and the junior and senior high schools are separated by double glass doors. I don't often have a reason, anymore, to be in the elementary part. But as I slide between the doors, I'm glad I came. I've entered another world—it's a trip back. Colored construction paper, taped to the walls, frames decorated poems entitled "What Is Spring?" Some little kid has pasted cotton balls onto brown crayoned lines to show that SPRING IS PUSSY WILLOWS!

I'm thinking about my second-grade teacher, Miss Huska. She had black hair and green eyes and I fell in love with her on the first day back to school after Christmas vacation. My dad had left on New Year's—packed up as much as he could get into his big brown suitcase and left for good, and even though I didn't know exactly what was going on, like that I wouldn't see him from then on except sometimes in the summer, I felt sad and sick. At recess, when everyone else went outside, Miss Huska let me stay with her, indoors. That was when I decided to invite her to have lunch with me.

In the smaller grades, the teachers would sit down and have lunch with a student if they asked. First you had to write out a formal invitation (to improve your writing skills), and then they would write back. When I handed her my invitation with a picture of a lady and a boy eating lunch in their bathing suits (beside a big sand castle), she laughed and said, "Thank you, Don. This is for *me*?"

She always said, "This is for *me*?" like you'd just handed her a million bucks.

After the bell rang, we all sat in our desks for art class. Miss Huska smiled when she gave me her reply, which read, "Dear Don: Yes, I will have lunch with you. Thank you for your gorgeous picture! And thank you for inviting me. Yours truly, Miss Huska."

That morning, in art class, I repeated in my mind the

word *gorgeous*, like a prayer, as I made her three lime green tissue-paper roses. She put them in her pencil can, where they stayed for months and gradually got faded by sunlight until we were let out for the summer.

Outside the second-grade room, which used to be Miss Huska's class, a boy is sitting in the hall, on a sunny spot, his legs sprawled. He's flicking his chewed-up pencil against his knee. The door is closed, but I can still hear the voice of his teacher on the other side, raving on about arithmetic.

I shove my hand into my jacket pocket. I feel the feather-light strings of the guitar. The kid looks really bored, waiting by the door until his punishment is over. I push against the toe of his shoe to get his attention. He's skinny, with a grown-out brush cut. I hand over to him my work of art.

He looks at it, turns it upright, raises his eyebrows like a TV cartoon. He smiles. He has the kind of teeth that'll need braces in a couple of years.

I'm beginning to wonder if he appreciates what I've just handed him. I remember reading somewhere that art doesn't become art until it goes out into the world.

"It's yours," I say.

Even as I say it, part of me wants to take it back. It looks better and better in his hands. I can't believe I've created something so . . . gorgeous. That I actually did that. Finally I say, testy as hell, "Do you want it, or don't you?"

The kid pulls it to his chest, and my heart sinks. Then he gives me the craziest wink and starts madly fingering that tiniest guitar in the world like he's some big-time rocker.

He gets so involved that he doesn't even notice me leave, my boots clacking down the hall.

Outside, the sun is bright and the air is cold. On my way through the school grounds, I pass the squirrel, on his back, forever playing the invisible guitar. I'm grateful to him. Maybe I should make more stuff out of rejected junk material—a sort of personal statement on over-looked beauty.

I lean over, touch my right hand to my forehead, and salute him. After that, I turn and head home into the strong spring wind.

The Kindness of Strangers ✝ ✝ ✝ ✝

In a telephone booth near the waterfront in Bemidji, Minnesota, Laker Wyatt takes the quarter, the one he panhandled from a tourist, from the zippered pocket of his sweaty leather jacket. The telephone booth smells of vomit, urine, and stale cigarette smoke, and Laker has left the door open. Still, the combination—hinting at shabby despair and regret—is almost more than he can stand.

He hasn't looked at himself in days. The last time was in a public toilet mirror—he can't remember where. It had scared him. He'd disappeared somewhere between then and three weeks before. His replacement was a haunted-looking stranger with stringy, greasy hair. It seemed a lifetime ago when he had withdrawn $120 from his now-defunct bank account, stuffed a few belongings and a gray wool blanket into a big army-green duffel bag, and then left home suddenly and finally. He took the first bus that was leaving for anywhere. Anywhere, as it turned out, was Bemidji.

Now he picks up the receiver, leans his head back, closes his eyes.

His mother was wearing a peach-colored bathrobe the morning he left. It was something one of their neighbors had lent her. She was getting bigger, the baby only three months away.

Her head is bent over a cup of coffee, and she's not looking at him. In spite of everything, she's still so blond and pretty.

"Why do you let him talk to you that way?" he says, appalled. "He comes home from one of his trips, and in five minutes he's got you crying. Why do you put up with it?"

"Laker, he's not a bad man." She puts her slender hand down flat on the table. "If you two could just get along a little better . . ." Her voice trails off.

He hesitantly reaches out and lightly places one finger on her back, tracing it slowly down her shoulder. She stiffens. He lets his hand drop.

"I've got to go," he says. But he waits.

"Right," she says, looking into her cup, searching for whatever it is he can no longer give her. "So go," she adds.

"Why did you ever marry him? Mom?"

She turns up this stony face she's taken to giving him ever since Rick the Prick muscled in on their lives. "Laker," she says, "will you just go?"

"Fine," he says in disgust. "Fine, I'm going."

He picks up his backpack and leaves for school. It's the last week before summer vacation. His last week in eleventh grade.

Later, when he comes home, he hears them arguing. His stepfather going on about how she forgot to get his beer when she was at the store.

"I just forgot," says his mother. "I'm sorry, okay?"

"Jesus, Audrey," he whines. "Didn't I ask you before you left? Just *before?*"

Laker walks into the kitchen. Rick is sagged over the table, chewing a sandwich. Chewing with his mouth open. He actually makes noises when he eats. This man is so beneath his mother, he should be begging at her feet for attention.

Instead, she's standing against the stove, her hand on her stomach, on that obscene baby that will be hers and his, drinking a glass of water. She quietly finishes it, her pale throat arched like a Swedish queen's. She sets the glass down on the counter and says, "I know you're tired. I'll go back."

"Don't do that, Mom," says Laker.

His mother shoots him a look.

"I said," says Laker as he stands between them, in the middle of the kitchen floor, "you don't have to go back to the store. Mom, don't go."

"So why don't you go, hotshot?" says Rick, opening his pack of cigarettes, flipping out the last one. "I'll pay you five bucks if you go get me a six-pack of beer."

"Screw you, asshole."

"Oh, right," says Rick, lighting his cigarette, exhaustedly shaking out the match. "Now he's calling me an asshole. Nice son you raised, Audrey." He picks up his sandwich with his other hand.

"I beg your pardon?" says Laker. "Don't talk to her that way. And what makes you such a Lord High Shit that you can make judgments on anything she does?"

"Laker, please," his mother pleads. "Stop this, right now."

"No, I mean it, Mom. He has no right. Look at him. Look at what you married. *Look . . . at him.* He has the manners of a pig."

"Pig?" Rick snorts. "That's nice, too. Oh, that's just peachy. Calling me a pig."

What made that moment so different from all the others? He has replayed it over and over in his mind. The bright kitchen light. The floor that always gleams with a high fresh polish. Rick's terrified face, the sandwich dropping from his hand as their bodies collide. Laker on top of him on the floor, his hands on that whiskered chicken-skin neck. And then the banging and banging and banging of Rick's head on the black and white tiles.

His mother has such thin arms. How did she manage to lift him off just like he was a five-year-old again?

Rick coughed and gagged, his face scarlet. His mother screamed, "Get out! Get out of here! Get out of this house—get out!"

For a moment he hoped she meant Rick. Then, unbelievably, he knew that she meant him.

Laker puts the quarter back in his pocket. He can't

face making the call home today. Maybe tomorrow. The hamburger he begged from the perky blond with the too-bright smile, outside wherever it was, is making him sick. Now all he wants to do is go lie down in the grass under some tree and sleep forever.

He weaves off, leaving the receiver dangling, and throws up outside the booth.

It's midnight. Top of another day. The phone booth affords the best view in Bemidji of the wooden statue of Paul Bunyan. Laker stumbles past Paul and his blue ox, goes in behind a clump of bushes, and lies down. He hides inside his jacket, grateful that it's so big and loose. He's paranoid that someone will steal it right off his body while he's sleeping. So whenever he finds someplace to lie down for a few hours, he does it all up—zipper, snaps, the works.

Hugging his arms around it and himself, he curls up into a tight ball with his head on his duffel bag. He shivers from exhaustion and from having been sick. Then he remembers, with an acute pang, that he lost his blanket somewhere near the amusement park. Was that yesterday? A big guy, wearing a red cap like Chucky's, just walked off with the blanket dangling like a serape down his back. And smiled over his shoulder. What a loser. His big front teeth just the same as Laker's old stuffed toy, Chucky the Beaver. Whatever happened to Chucky? He can't quite remember his bedroom, back then. Was it blue? Yes. That was it. And on the window ledges, lined up like good soldiers—all those books he used to read. One or two a night before he'd finally fall asleep.

Books. That last one he finished reading, holed up on

a rainy night in a Bemidji library (before a young librarian with an apologetic smile turned off the lights and said, "You can come back tomorrow"). The Tennessee Williams play. *A Streetcar Named Desire.* He thinks about the main character, Blanche Dubois. About that line that comes near the end of the play. A doctor has come to cart her away to the loony bin, and she's hanging on to his arm. "Whoever you are . . . ," she says, "I have always depended on the kindness of strangers."

He thinks about how, as he left, he could actually feel Blanche Dubois follow him out of the library into the steamy, downpouring rain. He slowed, feeling her presence behind him. She leaned against one of the white pillars, her blond hair drenched, her flowing summer dress clinging to her frail body.

That was last Friday. And here it is— Tuesday? Wednesday? So far, he's avoided being hauled off for vagrancy. He wonders how long his luck will hold out. Just lately he's begun to rely on handouts. He's fast becoming dependent on sympathetic librarians, the odd tourist, and all the cheerful Scandinavian Bemidji blonds (their tanned legs, clean white shorts, and throwaway snacks) who only a month ago would have given him their phone numbers.

He rolls over onto his back. The northern lights, spooky and shifting, have begun to dance and expand in the cooling night sky.

Next morning, as he's walking toward the Marketplace, he finds a ten-dollar bill. It flutters like a large green butterfly across Paul Bunyan Drive.

He buys two hamburgers and a hot apple pie and a jumbo cup of coffee with three sugars and four creams. Later he sees an elderly man, wearing suspenders to hold up his loose-fitting brown polyester pants. Standing under a canopy, surveying the early slanting sunlight, he gently licks away the tail end of an ice-cream cone. He seems to be waiting for someone.

Laker politely walks up to him, asking softly, "Can you spare some change, sir?"

"You should be working" is the grumbling reply. But a veined, slightly shaky hand searches a pocket of the polyester pants, pulls out a couple of broken toothpicks and a handful of change, pauses as the man deliberates how much to give. He hands over seven quarters, four dimes, and a penny. Eyeing the penny, he advises, "It'll keep you honest."

Weird old duck. "Yes, sir. Thank you, sir." Laker walks away, glad of the change. He carefully tucks that, with the remaining silver from the ten dollars, into the zippered pocket of his jacket.

The next day, it rains constantly. His shoes feel like sponges on his feet. His jacket is a chilled, damp misery against his bare arms. The rain that began in little drizzles early in the morning has, by mid-afternoon, started to shed huge, steady plops. People dash in and out of stores, in and out of water-beaded cars and trucks that pull in to park, pull out again, splash on by.

Near the doorway of Thriftway Drugs, he sinks to the sidewalk and sits on his wet duffel bag.

"I don't suppose another handful of quarters is going to help you over the long haul. Goddamn economy, it's got everybody down. Like the goddamn thirties in some ways. I've seen you around here quite a bit lately, and I've got to tell you that you have about as much eye appeal as a drowned cat."

Laker lifts a slow gaze from the sidewalk to the profile of the old guy from yesterday. He's staring off into the rain as he works away at his teeth with a toothpick. He's got on a green plaid fedora-style hat and an unbuttoned floppy yellow rain slicker and the same brown pants and suspenders.

"I hate this goddamn weather," he says. "Makes my arthritis seize up like crazy. And it makes me grumpy as hell. Damp cold—it's the worst."

"No kidding," says Laker dismally.

An old-model maroon Chevy, windshield wipers clapping back and forth, pulls up to the curb. The driver is a middle-aged woman in turquoise sweats and plastic earrings; she reaches over the passenger's side and flips open the door.

"That one's Vera Lynn," says the old guy. "Got two of them—kids, that is. My son's happily *un*-married and living in San Diego. But that one is married and miserable, bossy as hell. My wife died just over two years ago,   . and I've been henpecked ever since." He touches the brim of his hat. "Well, nice talking to you, then."

"Bye," says Laker. With lonely eyes, he watches the old guy ease himself into the car, then make two attempts before finally banging shut the passenger's door.

He gives Laker a quick appraising once-over as Vera Lynn pulls out from the curb. Gently swaying, the car splashes away through the puddles.

Not more than three minutes later, when the rain has slowed once more to a drizzle, Vera Lynn's car comes tearing back to the curb and lurches to a halt. The car rocks back and forth. The window on the passenger's side rolls down. The old man first sticks out a yellow rain-slickered elbow, then, stiffly, his head. "It occurs to me," he says to Laker (who has stood up out of sheer surprise). "It occurs to me," he repeats, then turns his head to his daughter. "Vera Lynn, turn down those goddamn whiny violins . . . thank you," and turning back to Laker: "It was my intention to phrase this properly, but evidently I am being rushed." Once again he turns to his daughter, who is saying something—Laker can't hear what. The old man interrupts her, "Vera Lynn, if this is too god-damn much trouble for you, then I will get out, right here, and walk home."

Laker wonders if he should move a little closer to the car but then remembers to remain neutral. Begging has its own rules. He's quickly learned that opportunities can blow either way. If you can manage to stand in the middle, somewhere between taking action and yielding to fate, then things sometimes work out in your favor.

"I live about a ten-minute drive from here," says the old man, finally addressing Laker. "Name's Henry Olsen. Do you do yard work?"

The rain patters softly all around them. Vera Lynn

rolls down her window a few inches. Her right hand still grips the top of the steering wheel.

"Yard work," says Laker. "You need yard work done?"

"Yep. Need quite a few things done. And then there's this tree branch the size of a hotel that's resting on my roof. Has to be trimmed back. Has to be done. I'll pay you"—he drums his fingers on the side of the car—"six dollars an hour. Is that fair?"

Yard work. He wants to hire an illegal underage hobo runaway to do yard work. Maybe he's an old pervert. Maybe he does this all the time. Or maybe he's just lonely as hell. "You need yard work done?" Laker repeats.

"That's what I just said. I'll give you cash, by the way. No checks. No questions asked. If you want to keep sitting on your hindquarters out here in the rain, that's your choice and none of my business. But it doesn't take a genius to see that you're getting nowhere fast."

Laker feels as if he's being shaken from a deep and troubling sleep. He tries to focus on all that is being asked of him, and it's a painful effort that stubbornly hooks him to the spot.

Henry Olsen stares politely away. "When you're ready," he says in a slow, patient tone, "hop in. And don't forget your gear over there."

It's been a long time since he had a shower, and that's the first thing Henry Olsen insists he do. It's a cluttered little house that smells faintly of coffee and wood smoke. Laker steps into the metal shower stall with a bottle of shampoo. The hot water blasts his skin and feels incredible as he washes away three weeks' worth of itchy dirt and trouble. He can't believe how luxurious it is to simply get clean.

The old man has lent him an old-fashioned gray sweat suit. Laker towels down and then puts it on, the warm fleece against his skin. Emerging from the steamy bathroom, he suddenly feels wobbly with exhaustion.

At the stove, Henry Olsen turns and says, "Washing machine's over there, in the corner." Written in green letters across the front of his white chef's apron is TRY A LITTLE TENDERNESS—THE PORK PRODUCERS.

"Vera Lynn," he announces, "went home in a tempestuous huff. Says I'm being foolish. Foolish for inviting a complete stranger into my home." It's a statement that seems to demand a response.

"I don't think you're being foolish," Laker says quietly. He sets down his duffel bag by the washing machine.

"Good. I'm glad you feel that way," says Henry Olsen. He's easing something white and flour-dusted into the pan. "I've got at least a couple of days' work waiting right outside for you to do. But not tonight. How do you feel about that?"

"That would be fine," Laker says gratefully.

"Good. I figure tomorrow's soon enough. Everybody's always in such a goddamn hurry."

Along with his rain-soaked clothes, Laker throws everything from the duffel bag into the washing machine. He then pours in a cup of detergent, closes the lid, and turns the dial to Wash. With an alarming rattle and a high-pitched whine, the machine suddenly shakes into action. He jumps back, afraid he's done something wrong. And then, surprisingly, it settles into a gentle churning cycle.

"Trouble with Vera Lynn is her blind obstinacy," says Henry Olsen, reflectively poking at the pan with a metal spatula. "She operates on the notion that anybody over seventy-five has nothing to contribute—not that she'd ever put it into so many words. No, no, she means to be kind. She'd blow your nose for you if you asked her. Works in a seniors' home. God help those poor old buggers over there. She's probably got them all organized into wheelchairs and diapers and songfests."

A buttery, peppery smell has begun to steam and bubble up. He continues, "Do you like panfried fish? Friend of mine, Frank Johanns, was up at Blackduck Lake yesterday. Best walleye in the world."

Laker straddles a kitchen chair, his arms folded along the smooth curved wooden back, and faces his host.

"Of course I don't drive anymore," says Henry Olsen. "Had an accident last year. After that I figured at eighty-two years of age, I'd had a pretty good run at it. Who wants to kill somebody just because they're too damn proud to know when it's time to give it up? I miss it, though. I surely do. Kissed off a good-size chunk of my independence, right then and there. Any that remains, my daughter is only too happy to take off my hands. Got your driver's license?"

"Yes," says Laker.

"Had it long?"

"Awhile."

"There's a few things I should know about you, son—like, for starters, your name."

He hesitates. "It's Laker." He pauses, and then he adds, "Wyatt."

"Your parents must really like basketball," responds Henry Olsen, quick as anything.

"My biological father does," says Laker with a slow smile. "Apparently I was conceived during an L.A. Lakers game."

"That a fact?" Henry Olsen chuckles, flipping over a crispy golden chunk of walleye. "That's one game he didn't get to watch." He turns down the element. "Does he still like basketball?"

"I don't know. He took off shortly after I was born. We hear from him once in a while. Never used to stay in any one place for too long. But I guess he's settling down now, because he's married and got a two-year-old kid."

"So where's your mother living?"

"Duluth," says Laker, and right away he realizes he's been caught off guard. Henry Olsen is an old snake charmer.

"So you're not too far from home, then. Could always go back if you wanted to." He carefully dishes the fish onto a platter, then sets it in the oven.

Laker blinks at the bright blue kitchen floor.

Henry Olsen nods sympathetically. "Life is full of suffering, son. Suffering is normal. How old are you?"

Might as well tell him. Sooner or later he's going to charm everything out into the open, anyway. "I'm sixteen. I'll be seventeen in four months," says Laker, trying to work up a little enthusiasm.

"Seventeen." Henry Olsen considers this. He pulls a couple of plastic food containers from the fridge, and he says, "See, there's this big difference between us." He brings the containers to the table, leans over, setting them down, then stiffly straightens up. "Unlike me, you've got a thousand more chances to start all over again with people."

Laker turns his head, resting his cheek on his arm. Out past the kitchen's modern sliding glass door, a door oddly out of keeping with the rest of the house, is an enormous old oak tree. The sun has finally come out and slants late afternoon gold, down Bemidji's summer sky. Backlit, a thick ancient-looking branch rises up over the roof of Henry Olsen's house. Thinner leafy branches protrude downward. Dangling from one is a child's wool mitten. It's bright red and dripping with rain.

The telephone rings, a black wall-phone by the doorway that leads into another room. Henry Olsen answers on the fourth ring.

"No, no," he's saying, "thanks for calling, but everything's just fine here. Yes . . . well, that's Vera Lynn for you. Sorry that she bothered you with this, Frank. Ever since her mother died, her diligence on my behalf has become an increasing pain in the ass. But today it occurred to me that I still have a mind of my own, and I guess it's high time we had a discussion about that. By the way, the walleye looks terrific. Just cooked it up. Say, thanks again for bringing it around."

"Well, well," says Henry Olsen, coming to the table with the rest of their supper.

"Do you mind," says Laker, "if I make a phone call before we eat?"

"Yes, I mind," says Henry Olsen. He wears half glasses, and he does a quick study of Laker's face before he loads up his plate with two pieces of walleye, a big spoonful of potato salad, and some marinated vegetables. "You should never make a rash decision on an empty stomach," he explains. "What's your hurry?"

"I don't know," Laker mumbles.

"Well, if you don't know, then you don't need to hurry. Eat."

Laker listlessly cuts off a corner of walleye.

"When's the last time you had a decent meal?"

"I don't know," says Laker. "I guess it was yesterday. Or maybe the day before. I don't remember."

"Fish is supposed to be brain food. What grade are you in?"

"Going into my senior year in high school. I guess."

"Listen, son, when you call that mother of yours, will you let me talk to her?"

Laker thinks about that time when he and his hippie mother were camping in a trailer park in Oregon. He remembers running away into the water in the fierce sunlight and her picking him up, his legs still kicking, and carrying him back to the beach. In those days, when he did something he wasn't supposed to, she'd usually scold him with a smile in the back of her eyes.

He stares at his plate, his hands resting on either side. His nervous fingers curl and uncurl. He hopes that Henry Olsen doesn't notice what a mess he's in, here at this table where kindness abounds.

Henry Olsen clears his throat, wipes his mouth with his napkin, then sets the napkin down. He reaches out a mottled, veiny hand and pats Laker's shoulder.

"Make your call, son," he says quietly.

So, he'll simply make the call. That's all he has to do. Tomorrow morning he could be back on the bus, this time heading home to Duluth. Maybe the old man will even lend him the bus fare.

Maybe things will be different this time. Maybe this time, her shell will crack and his real mother will step away from the tall, straight, hard-chiseled covering that hides her. She'll step away, laughing, and something about him will please her. Her eyes will soften. Her arm will ride easily along his back.

He pushes away from the table, gets up, walks across Henry Olsen's kitchen to the phone. He makes his call.

When she picks up the phone, the cord at the other end makes a familiar clinking sound. This means she's in the kitchen. The cord has passed across the fruit bowl, which is usually empty. He's pulled her away from her own dinner. She accepts the collect call, and then says, "Laker, where are you?"

"I'm in Bemidji."

"You're in Bemidji."

"And I want to come home."

"Laker . . ." She pauses, seems unable to continue, then quickly: "Rick and I have talked this over." She pauses again.

"Mom? I want to come home."

Has she turned to look at Rick, her gray-streaked blond hair falling over one eye?

The cord clinks again, over the bowl—the one he gave her two Christmases ago. It's the only recent thing he's given her that she's set out for the world to see. "The colors are nice," she said absently, and put it back in its wrapping. But later, it appeared on the table under the phone and has been there ever since.

"Laker," she says softly, "you can't live at home anymore."

I can't live at home. *Can't* live at home. He feels an overwhelming all-over cold, as if he's standing in a freezer. He's so numb, he's not sure if he can open his mouth to speak, and then, unbelievably, he feels these words forming in his mouth, foreign words as if some stranger inside his body has taken over and is about to speak for him. "Oh, that's all right," he hears this new voice say. "I didn't expect to, anyway. I was just phoning to find out how you were and if you needed anything."

He remembers bringing her tissues whenever she cried, making her supper when she couldn't get out of bed, calling into work—he must have been only ten years old at the time—to say that she couldn't make it in again today. No, not today, but maybe tomorrow.

"Well, Mom," Laker says. "I'm going to go now."

There's just silence at her end. Maybe she's crying. Who knows? Maybe Rick is there with his arm around her, holding her up, supporting her in this decision they have made together.

"I'll be in touch," he promises, and for just a few seconds, he waits. He waits for her to stand up for him. To tell him that she loves him. To ask him to come back. To tell him that they can still work things out. None of these things happens. Gently as a kiss, he sets the receiver back in its cradle.

He turns, comes back to the table, sits down.

"You can stay," says Henry Olsen firmly, then clears his throat, "for as long as it takes to get yourself together."

"That might be quite some time," Laker says quietly.

"I'm in no rush, son. Time is something I've got more of than I know what to do with."

The old man looks away, out the window. Laker follows his gaze to where the red mitten moves in a light wind. It spins one way, stops, then begins to unwind high in the arms of the huge old tree. He wonders about that bizarre perfect little mitten. He wonders how in the world it got there, and how it's managed, this far, to keep hanging on.

Where Has Romance Gone? + + + +

This morning, on the radio, I heard a journalist reporting from Russia. Behind her, in some café, young men and women danced to a slow jazz version of "Tea for Two." Here I am, applying my mascara, and suddenly I start bawling.

"It seems that women in Russia these days," the journalist was saying, "just want a little romance in their lives."

I heard that exact version of "Tea for Two" last summer. It came from the radio inside our cottage. I just happened to look up from the chaise. Past the pale summer screens, I could see my eighty-year-old grandparents. They were dancing.

He held her wrinkled hand just so—tenderly, against his heart. As they shuffled slowly around the living room, she turned her old eyes up and held him in her gaze.

I cried then, too. Cried because they were old and in love. Cried because there wouldn't be many more summers when they would dance together. Cried because they knew firsthand about something I don't think I will ever find.

I walk down the halls at school. Boys hover over girls at their lockers. That's where they're all at. And out on the street and in the malls, they play out their imitation of romance. They've bought the whole bill of goods that they see on the soaps or in cheap movies.

My last boyfriend, Tyler, who plays football, basketball, baseball, and spends the rest of his time in front of a mirror, told me, "Lindsay, you are just too analytical. Besides, you're looking for somebody to grow old with, when what you should be concerned about is having fun. With somebody like me!"

Tyler lasted three weeks, exactly. I couldn't get deeper than his toothpaste-ad smile.

After school and on weekends, I work in a music store. I get a 25 percent discount on everything I buy. To my collection I've added Beethoven, Chopin, the Red Hot Chili Peppers, the Doors, and the queen of the romantic jazz ballad, Sarah Vaughan.

Nobody my age has even heard of Sarah Vaughan. But, God, when she starts singing, "Drinking black coffee. Love's a hand-me-down brew," I know what she's talking about. I can feel it right down inside my shoes.

My mom says when she was growing up, men were often romantic and gallant and polite to their women. But then she just split with my stepfather, so she's probably feeling nostalgic.

These days, it seems, everyone has their own sad story to tell.

There's this guy who comes into the store sometimes. He looks as if he escaped from the sixties—he's all burnt out. He's going bald, and he wears his hair long, what's left of it, in a ponytail. He has this T-shirt with the American flag silk-screened on the back. I keep wondering if he's one of those guys who came up here to Canada during the Vietnam War. I don't think he ever got over the sixties. His hands shake so bad sometimes, and his face is pitted from too many drugs or something. Not exactly a romantic picture, but the guy is real. People look at him like he's a loser, but he's so polite. I have never met a more polite person.

He came into the store the other day, and I helped him find an old Rolling Stones tape.

"Thanks," he said, his eyes kind of glittery and red, "that's real nice of you." He has this twang, and his voice sounds as if somebody took an emery board to his vocal cords. He coughs a lot.

He turned over the cassette to examine the back. He squinted at all the song titles, then looked up and smiled. "I think maybe I'll take this one," he said. A large piece from the side of his tooth is missing, right at the front where it's really noticeable, but he has a sweet way about him.

"Take your time." I smiled over my shoulder as I turned and went back to the front desk.

Under the cheesy mustache he's trying to grow, my supervisor, Adam, said, "You talking to that old bum again? He never buys anything. The only reason he comes in here, Lindsay, is to check you out."

"Get serious," I said, taking a twenty from the woman who had been half an hour in the easy listening section.

Adam wandered off, shaking his head. "Touchy, touchy," he muttered.

These days we're not too busy in the store, so Adam and I stand up at the front and have pencil fights or just shoot the breeze. He's a nice enough guy, twenty years old, and he has a girlfriend he calls Conan the Destroyer. I have no idea why he continues to go out with her.

Tonight has been slower than usual. It's quarter after nine and almost time to close up the shop. Out in the mall, there's still the odd last-minute shopper. A lady with a big belly and crotch-splitting jeans and a dirty pale blue sweatshirt drags by with a kid in tow, a little boy who is about two or three. He's in a ratty yellow sweat suit, and he's yelling in frustration over something. He starts to cry. It's an angry cry—pretending heartbreak.

His mother just keeps hauling him along like he's this heavy growth on the end of her hand, some unhappy little burden she can't get away from. He's crying in earnest now, sobbing. She looks dead tired. I don't know who I feel sorrier for—her or that baby who's got a head start on misery.

The hippie suddenly appears with a little off-to-the-side cough. He's wearing his usual T-shirt, except you can't see the American flag on the back because he's wearing a brown windbreaker over the top. His hair is wet and looks skimpier than usual. Little dark spots of rain speckle his jacket.

Adam glares at him, flips his pencil in the air, catches it, and says, "We're closing."

"In fifteen minutes," I add with a smile and a tromp on the top of Adam's dull Loafer with one of my Le Château flats.

"I won't be long," the hippie says to me, nodding like he's just walked into a church.

"You just let me know if you need any help, now," I call after his wet jacket. His shoulders twitch slightly.

I turn to Adam. "Why are you so damn mean?"

"I'm not."

"Yes, you are." I slide past, giving him a solid bump with my hip that throws him off balance.

"Lindsay, Lindsay." His sharp laugh ends in a chuckle. "Go on and help your flower child."

He is gently flipping through the Doors tapes.

"Hi," I say in a lowered voice, so I won't startle him. "Jim Morrison, huh?" I pick up one of the tapes and lean my back against the tape rack. "They made a movie about him."

"I was at one of his concerts once," he says in his quiet, raspy way, not looking up.

"Wow. Impressive."

"It was," he says. "It really was."

"Where was that?" I don't want to seem like I'm pry-
ing, but I really want to know. He's such a mystery man,
this guy.

"San Francisco, in another life."

"Yeah? You lived there?"

"No. I went looking for this girl. *The one.*" With a soft
smile, still examining the tapes, he adds, "Do you know,
she had a light around her that you could actually see?
Yes, she did."

"And did you find her?"

He doesn't answer. With a little shiver, he zips up his
jacket. "You work here a lot," he says, finally looking at
me, his eyes wandering up past my forehead.

"Evenings. Weekends." I'm beginning to feel a little
weird.

"Enjoy it?" he asks me.

"It's okay."

"Got a dream?" he says, right out of the blue.

"Oh—sure," I stammer.

"What is it?" he asks in a flat voice, back flipping
through more tapes.

It's an honest question. But how do you come out
and tell a complete stranger, without sounding totally
flaky or giving him the wrong impression, that your dream
is to find some sincere person who'll cherish and romance
you?

He pulls out another Doors tape, turns it over, looks
up sideways at me in a shy way. He has incredible brown
eyes. "Sorry if I touched a nerve," he says softly. "Didn't
mean to do that to you, beautiful child."

I'm getting the strangest feeling. Goose bumps are rising up all along my arms. "Is—that what you called her?" I stammer. "The girl. With the light around her."

He fingers the tape, puts it back with the others, slowly nods. "I called her lots of things. Queen of Sheba . . . goddess . . . lady . . ."

"It's five minutes to closing," Adam calls out from the front of the store.

"She had this light, see? But I was the only one who noticed it. That's the thing of it. Do you believe in miracles?"

"Miracles?"

"I can see that you don't. Okay . . . I'm going to tell you this one thing, and then I'll say good-bye and go. You look like her."

"I look like her?"

"Yes, you do. You bear an eerie resemblance. First day I came in here, I thought I'd seen a ghost. Then I had to come back again, just to make sure. You aren't her, of course. You're just a girl working in a store, and I'm just a guy who came in out of the rain. But I have to tell you, just looking at you has made me feel better than I've felt in a long time. You take care of that light of yours."

He quickly turns and walks away. His stringy wet pony-tail is done up with one of those black elastics with the little gold flecks, and I don't know why I'm thinking this, but I have the oddest feeling I'll never see him again.

"You've got to be careful of guys like that," says Adam, coming up to me. "Sometimes they're weird. Really, really weird."

"Everybody's *really, really* weird, Adam," I say, looking up at him, a laugh catching in my throat. I rub my arms. "You're shaking," Adam says, alarmed. "What did that guy say to you? Lindsay?"

He puts an arm around me in a kind of brotherly way. He peers down into my face. "Ohhh, it's okay," he says, pulling me against his black-and-red sweater. He hugs me close and rocks me a little. "Are you okay, Lindsay? Are you okay?"

I just sink into his chest, my face against his soft, comforting sweater, and I don't say a word.

After that, I pull on my coat and go out into the rain. My mom's car is parked outside the mall, glistening cleaner than when I left it five and a half hours ago. The parking lot is almost empty, and the car rolls out into the street with rain drumming on the roof. I put on the wipers and roll down the window a bit so I can smell the rain.

I push a tape into the tape player, and as soon as I do, there's Sarah Vaughan: "It's not the pale moon that excites me, that thrills and delights me. Oh no, it's just the nearness of you."

She died a few years ago. She was sixty-six years old. Well, the angels really got something when they got her. Her voice was one of those pure gifts you run across only once in a very long time.

As the rain pelts down on the roof of this car, there she is inside her song, inside her life in 1949. She's sitting on a high stool behind a microphone. Maybe she's singing her song for some drummer. Or maybe she's singing for someone who is lost in the shadows of the sound booth.

Or maybe, just maybe, she's singing for some stranger who hasn't yet been born.

Inside this car, inside my life, I am listening. It's as clear as day that this woman's miraculous song is just for me.

The Ones with Wings -+- -+- -+- -+-

Her name is Mrs. Lacoste, and her tits are baggy under
the brown sweater she always wears. She never talks to
us when we stop by on our way home from somewhere.
She'll never look at you when she hands you your change.
I'm shivering in my grayish-that-used-to-be-pink sweatshirt and thin ski jacket, and she never so much as gives
me a smile, although she usually has a small down-eyed
one for my sister.

Selena, she's three years younger than me and small
for fourteen because she didn't grow much after that man
jumped up and down on her back, that man who used to
be our mother's boyfriend.

"Thank you, Mrs. Lacoste," says Selena, her pretty
lips parting in a smile when the woman hands her her
bag of chips.

She nods at Selena, then her eye catches her husband,

Dougy, in his shiny wheelchair. He is trying to move over a big box.

"*Gerald!*" she barks out their seven-year-old's name. "Go help your dad with that."

Gerald runs over, kicks the box, and keeps on running. Dougy rears back his head and laughs and laughs. Gerald has a great big sticky candy grin.

Selena makes like she's going to go over and help move the box, and that's when I tug on her sleeve to remind her of her back. She stops, gives me a dirty look, rips open her bag of chips, and limps out the door.

I look back at Dougy Lacoste. He's grabbed Gerald up onto his knee. The two of them go racing down the canned goods aisle in Dougy's wheelchair. Gerald hollers at the top of his lungs and makes passes at the whizzing-by floor with a string mop.

I go outside into the cold air. Selena is waiting for me. I'm still smiling about Gerald and Dougy.

Selena is not smiling. "Why do you always *humiliate* me?" she says, her shiny hair falling out of her hood.

I walk down the street after her. I don't know what else to do.

Occasionally I've stolen things for us, but they were small items to help us along—like school supplies for Selena because she's smart and personal items like deodorant and toothpaste and small boxes of tampons. But I try to get by without stealing. I have never stolen a thing from the woman at the corner. I go over to Safeway, where the cashiers smile at everybody. They just whip everything through, except for what you've got, there, hugged up inside your jacket.

I personally have never got caught, and I believe that's because God is mostly on my side. It's true. He tells me what's right and what's wrong. When I'm scared, I listen hard until he says, "Don't steal, Alvina, but if you have to, just once in a while and for a good reason, then I'll be busy watching somebody else at the time." He's like the father I have never had.

I started taking care of Selena when she was seven years old, and except for things that happened that weren't our fault, we haven't looked back since. Our mother has tried to do the best she can for us, but she's a weak woman. She lets things happen that shouldn't, and she's going to be on welfare all her life. Not like Selena. She's got ambitions.

I wish I was smart, like her, but then we've all got our crosses to bear. Just like Jesus, God's sorrowful son.

If Jesus is God's son, I guess that makes me Jesus's sister. That means that every church I go by is sort of like my house, too. But the one down on the corner of Lilia and Silton whose windows look like rubies and emeralds and sapphires and all kinds of other jewels— that's the one I go to.

The last minister of the church looked like God himself, every Sunday morning, as he stood by the doors when everybody walked out to go down the steps. He even had white hair. Except he never laughed. Two months ago, they got a new minister who laughs all the time, and that's when I started to go to church on a regular basis.

She has red hair and freckles, and she looks like a grown-up copy of Orphan Annie from the movie *Annie*, which Selena and I saw once, a long time ago. Her name is even Ann. Reverend Ann Parker—it's right on the sign outside the church. But in my mind I call her Annie. She drives a little green car with a sticker in the back window that says HONK IF YOU LOVE JESUS. She wears dark blue a lot, which, with that red hair of hers, all long and frizzy and just a little bit tied back so that it still flies around in the wind, doesn't hide the fact that she likes to have as much fun as she can, and that's not so easy with a job like the one she's got.

Selena never goes to church, but I keep asking her.

We get home. It's Saturday night. Our mother is already out somewhere. Now I will make us up some macaroni and cheese with ketchup. Later, we'll find a movie on TV and have tea with lots of sugar and milk and a bowl of popcorn.

Selena sulks off to our bedroom. "I'm going to sleep," she says.

"But it's only seven o'clock!"

"I'm going to sleep," she says again, and she closes the door.

Last Saturday, Selena told me I was quaint. Quaint? Now, that was another new big word for her. When I asked what she meant by that remark, she said, "You're very very very old-fashioned."

I sniffed and told her, "One *very* is enough."

"I mean it," she said. "Eighty-year-old ladies have more fun than you do. You're seventeen, Alvina. How come you act so boring?"

"It's from looking after you," I shot back. Right away I wanted to bite my tongue off. What a thing to say to the person you love best in the world.

Sunday morning I get up, and Selena doesn't open her eyes. So first I get ready for church, and then I try, again, to get her to go with me. I sit beside her and poke her awake.

She takes a loud breath, and her arm comes out from under the covers. She dances her fingers around for her glasses on the floor by our bed. She finds them, pushes them on, and looks at me. "I've never been to church," she says, before I've even asked her. "Why should I start going now? Alvina, I've never even been baptized. Why do you want me to go there?"

"I want you to go. Come on, now. Please get up." I'm playing with my thumbs as I sit there on the edge of the bed, all dressed up in my blue skirt and my white sweater that comes right past the bones on my wrists. I'm thinking that if she only went, maybe things would get better again, between us.

Selena carefully turns onto her back and stares at the crack in the ceiling where some plaster hangs like a big sore lip. In the next room, our mother coughs. It's the cough she always has on Sunday morning after she's been out on a Saturday night drunk. Sometimes there's a man in bed with her. Which is something I never want to know.

"I have a science test to study for, for Monday," Selena says. "I've got a history project that's due on Tuesday. Let me get some sleep."

She's in ninth grade, right where she should be. I'm in a special class for slow learners. Zip, zip—information comes whamming at my head in my special class. Sometimes I catch some, which is why I've got this far.

"Okay, I'm going," I say to Selena in a this-is-your-last-chance voice.

"Fine," she says, pulling her pillow up to her face.

I put on my jacket. I stand at the foot of the bed for a while, hoping Selena will change her mind.

"Why are you looking at me?" she says into her pillow.

"I'm not," I say.

"Yes, you are. I always know when you're looking at me. So just stop it."

"You don't want to go?"

She pulls the pillow off her face. She lies there deep in her bed. I am shocked to see big tears rolling down from the sides of her eyes. How is it that I've made her cry?

"Alvina," she says softly, "I love you very much. But I need to be on my own without you always looking at me like a sad old woman."

"I'm not a sad old woman," I say in an angry voice that makes me sadder than I can hardly understand. "I laugh sometimes. I laugh a lot, in fact."

"But you never laugh with me. With me it's all serious and hard work. It's like you just keep putting more and more heavy bricks on my chest. And I can't breathe."

She pulls up her pillow and sobs and sobs, and there is nothing I can tell her that will make her sadness go away, nothing I can tell her that will make her know I just want to do a good job and show her how much I love her.

It's a cold cold day, and the sky looks smeared and gray, and the air smells like it could use a good cleaning.

I walk around the corner and cross the windy street at the red light because no cars are coming. At the church, cars are parked up and down the street and last-minute latecomers are walking up the steps. I hang back and pull a half-eaten chocolate bar out of my pocket. I go and stand a little to one side under one of the glory windows, near the steps, and listen to the music coming out as I nibble a row of chocolate and peanuts away from the center of the bar. I save the rest, which I tuck back in the wrapper. I slide it into my pocket and wait a bit longer.

After about ten minutes, I walk up the church steps and open one of the heavy brown doors that seem to reach for heaven. I step onto the blue carpet.

There's Ray, in a heavy baggy suit, standing by the doors at the inside of the church. He is holding pamphlets and waiting. I can see all the way down to the altar. The people are settling down, and Annie's up there at the front with her robes on.

Ray is the only person from my special class who goes

to this church. He is the only one in my special class who feels like a friend. Today I need a friend.

Ray says, happy to see me, "Last one in. As usual."

"That's right," I say.

"You look sad today, Alvina."

"That's right," I say.

"Well," he says, tucking his big hand gentle as a heart under my elbow. Ray has hair that's red like Annie's. He has a funny kind of walk that's just Ray. I can tell it's Ray a mile off.

He ushers me in. He does this every Sunday, like I'm some sort of queen. He leads me down the aisle, and people always turn and smile at us. I get to sit in my favorite spot, always, right in the front pew, right in front of Annie, where I can almost smell that sweet, warm perfume she always wears.

When we are seated, Annie smiles at us.

Today, with Ray's shoulder hugged against mine, I think about Mrs. Lacoste at the corner, who never laughs, and Dougy, who always does, wheeling around with his son on his knee. We all do the best we can. I wonder if Selena went back to sleep. I wonder if she is dreaming some nice dream. After church I will go home and apologize for putting bricks on her chest. I shut my eyes as Ray breathes beside me. It's nice to know he loves me. It's nice to know that God and Annie love me. And everybody here in this church. We are all his angels. We are lighter than clouds.

The Northern Lights Theater Express ✠ ✠ ✠ ✠

I see him up in the school library with all his new friends. My used-to-be best buddy, Paul. They're all hanging out around a table—passing little foil packages to one another right under the table. His eyes have that wild-man look, like he's wired on something.

"Look at this," he says, coming up to me, flipping his crazy fingers at the collar of my Guatemalan shirt. "Where'd you get this, Jacko?"

My name is Jake. He used to call me Jack.

"Keep your hands off me."

"Ouch!" he says, shaking his fingers.

"You're such a loser." I say it with the James Dean squint I have perfected.

He focuses on my nose. His eyes are red, watery. He takes a deep breath and exhales, "Faggot."

"Don't fight the feeling, Paul," I say loud enough for

the whole library to hear. "Why don't you just go ahead and give me a nice big wet one?"

I stand there, like the idiot I really am, kind of barricading the library turnstile because I've gone so far in this charade I don't know what the hell else to do. And that's when he pops me one.

Let's stop the action. Right here.

The theater-school production that Paul saw me in, the one that started it all? It's opening night of the Northern Lights Theater Express's winter collective. There's a scene where my character, Dave, a real straight-acting guy, is shooting pool with his buddies, who are going on about this guy they all know named Jason. They're saying what a fag he is. Dave—that's me—spends the whole scene listening to them talk like homophobic redneck jerks about Jason, who is his secret lover, while he slowly circles around the table knocking balls into the side pockets.

Playing a gay guy was a terrific challenge. And it also scared me, especially with Paul sitting in the audience on opening night.

I go out to the lobby, after, to thank everybody for coming to the production. My mother hugs me, smelling of Hermès perfume, and looks anxiously into my face. I laugh because, once again, I've convinced her. She hugs me again and laughs in real delight and pats my back, and we sway each other around until I practically lift her off the floor.

And then there's Paul, standing with his hands in his pockets, looking totally squirmy.

"I'm an actor. What can I say?" I give him a playful shove.

He actually winces. "Weird, man," he says, backing off with a forced laugh.

"Get used to it," I tell him, with perfect seriousness. "It's the new me."

I don't know what made me say it. Maybe it was partly because I was just so tired of him always having the upper hand. And maybe it was partly because I was looking for a reaction. I'm always looking for a reaction. That's one of the reasons I like being an actor.

The reaction was staggering. Paul stopped being my friend, and right after that, the rumors started.

Anyway, here I am in the library. My nose is bleeding, and I've hit my head on the corner of the checkout desk. Mr. Remillard, the head librarian, and Jessie Green, a twelfth-grade library aid, come rushing up and stand over me. I catch their concerned looks and the flaming glow of Jessie's hair and her big beautiful body, just before I take off out of the library.

Let's quickly pan the camera to last year. Eleventh grade.

Paul and I are doing stand-up comedy in the halls. People hang around and throw quarters into our gym bags. Our mascot, a stuffed crocodile named Ace that we drag everywhere on a chain, is snugged against my feet.

This absolutely incredible six-foot-tall girl comes swaying toward us. I see her in the hallways every day. She always dresses completely in black and wears an enormous ruby in her nose.

People, as usual, start to notice her more than us. Three short skinny girls in practically identical tops start doing their oh-my-Gaaaaawd routine. A couple of guys give her a weirded-out once-over and then take off down the hall, hooting and carrying on like morons.

This time the girl stops. She throws her backpack down beside me. She gives Ace a little punt with her boot. With a tense smile, her sad, flat eyes flickering from Paul to me, she says, "This is my locker. Okay?"

I want to smile back, even though she scares me. I like her courage. I like the way she doesn't seem to give a damn about the reactions of the rest of us: closed up, scared, and lonely in our little safe routines.

But I don't smile. Instead, because Paul, like the rest of them, thinks she's a fat freak—I know he does, I can tell by his disgusted look—I jump back like she's a tank about to run over me.

She gives me the finger.

The girl whom I have just described is big, beautiful Jessie Green. Now library aid. Jessie Green with her maniac cloud of soft red hair. She's larger than life. To my way of thinking, she's voluptuous. To the generic you-have-to-be-stick-thin-to-fit-in consciousness of North American society, she's fat.

Paul's control over my personal tastes started back in seventh grade. I'd just moved up to Winnipeg, a Canadian prairie city of over half a million, from the North Dakota town where I'd grown up and where nothing, I mean absolutely nothing, ever happened. Paul was the first guy I met at my first day at school. We shared a locker. That first day we also shared my lunch because Paul had forgotten to bring his.

"What's this?" he says, opening like a wide, obscene mouth the sandwich half I've so generously handed him.

"Peanut butter and banana."

"No, *this*! This white junk! What *is* this!"

He says it so loud, half the cafeteria is looking at us.

"It's mayonnaise," I say, embarrassed.

"Mayonnaise?"

Paul falls to the floor, dying, his legs twitching uncontrollably. His performance is so convincing that a couple of teachers stand up to see what's wrong, their chairs crashing backward. And then he suddenly sits up like a jack-in-the-box, smiling at everybody.

After that moment, a couple of things happened. One, I stopped eating my favorite sandwich in public. Two, I started to act like a comedian at school.

Okay, let's go back to the library of E. L. Fairbourne High School and Mr. Remillard's skinny legs as he runs out the double doors after me.

"Jake!" he calls. "Jake! Wait!"

But I'm not waiting for Remillard, or anybody. I'm flying.

By the time I pull up to the curb at the older two-story house that Mom and her partner, George, have remodeled into their store, I'm calm. I'm strangely calm. I walk inside, and the familiar smell of lavender incense reaches a far corner of my olfactory nerve. I sneeze, wipe my nose with my hand. I'm still bleeding! I pull a tissue out of the box behind the cash register and am just wiping my face when Mom, dressed in a flowing gray caftan with matching pants, turns from the customer she's been waiting on.

One delicate eyebrow lifts up. She had me when she was nineteen, so is the youngest mom of just about anybody I know.

"My God," she says, coming over, "what's happened to you?" We are practically chin to forehead. She's a short woman.

She has the good sense not to embarrass me by touching my face. The customer, a blond executive-type with big earrings and wearing a purple suit, is staring at us. Mom puts her hand on my back and steers me into the back room. There, beside a diamond-studded blue evening gown marked SOLD, she fixes me with a solemn brown-eyed stare.

"It was Paul, Ma," I say, because she's always cornering me into telling the truth.

"What inspired him to hit you?"

"I don't know." I glance away, look quickly back, and add, "Nothing."

"Nothing? Just look at your poor nose."

"I've got a chemistry test this afternoon. What am I going to do?"

"I'll call your principal and cover for you."

"Do you think it's broken?"

"Why did he hit you?"

"Do you think it's broken, or not? I want to know."

"Go to the walk-in clinic," she says, not taking her worried eyes off mine. "Then go home and lie down. Listen to your Tibetan monk chants or something. I'll be home in good time tonight."

"My life sucks," I tell her sadly.

She places her small, thin hand on my shoulder. "Have a little faith," she says—as much, I think, to herself as to me.

At the clinic, a doctor with a hollow chest and pouchy eyes and bad breath examines me and tells me to put an ice pack on my nose, which he says isn't broken.

I go home and locate a bag of frozen peas in back of the freezer. I apply this to my nose. Then I open a can of spaghetti and share it with my cat, 'Shroom. It was Paul who named him, one winter day two years ago when we found him shivering behind a Dumpster, gnawing on a piece of frozen vegetarian pizza.

'Shroom is not an especially handsome cat. He has this spacy look, because one of his eyes is slightly crossed and the other doesn't exactly look right at you. It gives him a certain meditative, trancelike appearance—sort of like Bob Marley, after a lot of ganja.

And he's really good company. He eats anything. Drinks anything. Likes all my music. Doesn't complain when I turn on the TV. Minds his own business. He likes me better than anything else—except his food bowl.

I slip into my own numbing trance with the frozen peas on my nose while the TV drones on about cars and deodorant and contestant number two winning another four hundred bucks if he can only guess how many keys there are on a piano. That's when the telephone rings.

"Hi," I say in a bored, ticked-off tone, noting that a piano has eighty-eight keys. Should have known that.

"Hello," says a soft, lush voice. "Is this Jake?"

I sit up quickly, swinging my right leg off the back of the sofa, making 'Shroom squirm into an indignant huddle at the far end.

"This is Jessie Green," says the voice.

"Oh, Jessie, hi. How's it going?" I say casually, like she calls me up all the time.

"How are *you*?" she says, concerned.

"Fine. I guess. So. How's the library?" I'm nodding like a fool. I *am* a fool. Thank God she can't see me!

"I saw what happened to you," she says, with this sad, incredible little sigh.

I can't speak. I get this image of her sighing. Her breasts are large and round. Her hips are large and round. Her legs are a million miles long. Take a look at the movie goddesses of the fifties. Marilyn Monroe. Jayne Mansfield. Take a long, hard look. These were not small, thin, starved-looking women. They ate well. Probably licked whipped cream out of things. They had great tongues. Probably agile enough to take a cherry stem and tie it in a knot inside their mouths. I'd love to see that. It would drive me crazy. I've never met a girl who could do that.

"Jake? Are you still there?"

"Yes! I'm still here. I just dropped something." I lean

over and rattle a newspaper so she'll think I really did, and then flick off the TV so I can hear her voice better.

"I just want to say," she continues, "that I have an uncle who's gay and he's my favorite uncle and we have a terrific time together and I think Paul is a total jerk for tormenting you the way he's been doing. Did you know he could be expelled for punching you? Mr. Remillard is so upset. I *hate* this school! You can't imagine how hard it is to get out of bed every morning."

She suddenly stops dead. Like a motor that's seized. Like she's got started and is afraid of losing total control so she's put a choke on it.

"Mr. Remillard thinks," she continues in a restrained voice, "that it's just awful the way Paul's been treating you since—you know. Since you came out."

My head is reeling.

'Shroom cleans his paws, making loud slurping noises. He nibbles away with his teeth on the underpads and pulls out a little burr from between his toes. He spits it onto the Icelandic throw rug that's barely covering my right foot.

"Well," says Jessie, after a long, terrible pause, "I just wanted you to know I was thinking about you. Call me sometime. If you want to."

"Jessie," I blurt out, "I'm not gay."

"Oh," she says, hesitating.

There is a pencil beside the phone. I pick up this week's *TV Scene*. On the cover, there's a photo of some actress in a red dress with bare arms and a cheesy smile. "Okay," I mumble, "what's your number?"

As Jessie reels off the numbers, I tattoo them to Cheesy's shoulder. Then I start to draw Dracula fangs over her cheesy capped teeth.

"Have you got that?"

I wish she'd just go. Just leave me alone to sink down again, inside my misery.

"Are you there? Jake?"

"No," I say sarcastically, "I've disappeared."

"Jake," she says, "do you like old movies? Do you like James Dean?"

"He's okay."

James Dean is my idol. He's taught me everything I know about acting, even if he is dead. He's like this *primo* Method actor. Him and Marlon Brando and Monty Clift . . .

"I *love* James Dean," Jessie enthuses. "Did you know that"—she falters, then starts again—"did you know that *Rebel Without a Cause* is playing at Cinema Three this week? Have you ever seen it?"

"I've rented it a couple of times." Eleven, to be exact. I've memorized most of his lines. "I wouldn't mind seeing it again."

"You wouldn't? Because, you know, how many people our age ever get to see it on a big screen? James Dean, larger than life—just as he was in 1954."

"1955," I correct her. "The picture was released just after he died."

"Right! That's right! Everybody I know," she says softly, "has such poor taste in movies."

In the kitchen, the refrigerator starts to hum. Outside our condo, down on the street, is the grayest spring day you've ever seen. The half-eaten can of spaghetti, on the coffee table, with the congealing red sauce dripping down one side, is a depressing sight. I hate canned spaghetti. Especially cold, which is the way Paul likes it. Maybe this girl just needs a friend. Maybe if I stay here, my back will form tentacles and grow me into the sofa. Maybe I don't know what I want anymore, or feel, or care about. Maybe I don't even know who I am.

"Where do you live?" I hear my voice say. "What time do you want me to pick you up?"

I crash out on the sofa for a couple of hours. Then I get up, shower, and examine my nose in the mirror. It passes, thank God, for normal. As I'm leaving, I write a note to Mom telling her that I'm going out to a movie and that my nose isn't broken. Then at the bottom in big letters I write: YOU WERE RIGHT ABOUT HAVING A LITTLE FAITH. I THINK. LOVE YOU, MA. SEE YOU LATER. JAKE.

She'll wonder what the hell is up. But she respects my privacy. She won't ask why unless I tell her.

The first thing I notice when Jessie steps into the car is that she's wearing odd-looking shoes. They're kind of orthopedic looking. She catches me staring at them.

"I have bad ankles," she says, flicking back her hair. "I have to wear them for support. I used to wear boots, but now I wear these. We all have to grow up sometime."

I remember the boots. I remember the way she used to

dress all last year. The pungent perfume that screamed, "Back off!" When did she change? I can't recall. It was so gradual. First it was a blue sweater instead of the black turtleneck. Next she stopped wearing bright lipstick. I mean, she always was a knockout, even in her dramatic days, but she's changed so much.

She has on a sweetish musky perfume. It's really womanly. She smells different from other girls. And I get this feeling coming from her. It isn't that walloping sadness anymore, which used to follow her around like a shroud. Whenever she'd walk into a classroom, the atmosphere would suddenly change. People would shoot one another secret knowing looks.

No, now there's more of a warm, dull ache, the kind that I catch sometimes from certain people. It starts in the middle of my body, and it always dances up and out from there—like the northern lights when they shift and disappear and reappear somewhere else. The feeling leaves through my lips, my fingers, sometimes even through my toes. And it leaves me tingling. And it makes me feel weird. I think it may mean that I'm crazy.

But then I'm an actor, an artist. Artists are supposed to be crazy, right? A little eccentric, sensitive. We notice things, hidden behind the appropriate masks we wear.

We drive to the movie theater, which is about twenty minutes from Jessie's house, without saying a word. I feel nervous and off balance. She's wearing a skirt. There are golden freckles on her knees and all down her long long legs to the tops of her strange brown shoes.

When we step inside the tiny theater, there are only two other people in the lobby, a man and a woman. They loiter around, reading from a small stack of university newspapers.

"Looks like we're the only ones here," I say.

"It's sometimes like this," Jessie tells me. "During the week, not too many people come here."

As I pay the lady in the booth, Jessie adds quietly, "I want to be a filmmaker."

"Really." I'm nodding in a stunned manner. This girl is full of surprises.

We walk inside. There are only two other couples. Two thirds of the way down, Jessie slips through the row and stops right in the middle.

Just before we sit, something flashes in my mind to look back at the couple in the side aisle. I look. It's Trish Hall and Andy Fletcher, a couple of snots from E. L. Fairbourne's drama class. This was the class I flunked out of because I stopped going. That was just before I got serious about acting and joined Northern Lights. Jessie looks back to see who I'm looking at and then turns to face the screen like someone just pointed a gun at her head.

"You're beautiful," I tell her. Just like that. Just following my instincts for the first time in a long while.

She starts fiddling with the drawstring on her purse.

It occurs to me that no guy has ever told her this. It also occurs to me that I have to put my money where my mouth is. So in this very public place, with all the lights on, I touch her chin, and before she can pull away, I lean in and plant a kiss, like a flower, on her beautiful astonishing mouth.

The lights go off; the projector comes on. There are no previews. No dumb ads. Just the movie. Just the real movie in its original untampered-with color. WAR-NERCOLOR flashes across the screen. And immediately there's the man himself. James Dean. He's lying on a midnight street in this most famous of all scenes. And he's drunk as a lord, holding up a small toy, squinting his famous squint.

You've Always Been Such a Good Friend to Me ✝ ✝ ✝ ✝

My cousin Niki used to be the prettiest girl you ever saw. Silky hair the color of burnt caramel and a figure that workmen from the seventh floor of a construction site could tell was closer to heaven than they were.

Now she's so thin you could ease her sideways through a sheet of plywood. And she's dyed her hair a fried-egg yellow because Randy—that's her sleazebag husband— is cheating on her with the greasy blond waitress at the Husky Gas Station and Coffee Shop, where he works on weekends.

She loves her kid—I'll say that for her. But what sort of chance does it have, with a seventeen-year-old mother who has a ninth-grade education and a father who's never home? He tells her that what he does on his own time is between him and the wall, seeing as how he's providing a roof and groceries for her and little Kristel. Randy is ten years older than Niki and just an old-fashioned guy.

He brags to his buddies at his regular job at Fulton Trucking—where I work after school three evenings a week—about robbing the cradle when he married Niki. Interesting term, *robbing the cradle*. All the time, when people are robbed, they say they feel violated. Raped, in a manner of speaking. And what I am talking about here is rape, as in the rape of Niki's soul.

Who Niki was, a couple of years ago, can now scarcely be found. It's as if she's hidden herself. You know how you might break something on the floor, clean it up, and get a glass sliver in your hand? Just try to find it. Even under a strong light, it gleams only once in a while. That's Niki. Sometimes I catch her inside gleam when she smiles at Kristel. If she stays with Randy, I swear one of these days, it'll disappear altogether.

But Randy still has this hold over her. He is the founder of the let-me-throw-you-over-my-shoulder school of seduction. That's how he got Niki in the first place. He actually carried her, like that, out of a school dance. For weeks after, that's all every girl at John Preston High School talked about. And I guess you could say that I was one of them.

Last Thursday, I was late for work. Shivering, I pulled off my coat as the phone was ringing off the hook. Randy comes in from the loading dock.

"Great sweater," he says, sliding his hand down my back. "I'm goin' to the coffee machine. Want a cup?"

"No. I don't."

"Got any change?"

I pick up the phone, cradling it to my ear, and rifle through my backpack. I hand him fifty cents, which I know he won't pay back. A lady at the other end of the line wants to ship a sofa bed to her son—a teacher at Snow Lake.

Randy's buddy Kent leans over the order desk, dropping cigarette ashes onto a pile of pink freight slips.

"Kent," I say, "can you take your cigarette somewhere else?"

"Yeah, Kent," says Randy, coming back with a steaming cup of murky coffee. "Don't you have something else to do?"

Kent looks at him, then at me, lets out a snort, and gently stubs his cigarette in the square ashtray somebody lifted from the A & W at the corner. He zips up his jacket and goes.

Randy smiles and leans in on me. I whisper, "Piss off," right into his startled face.

Randy doesn't know the meaning of rejection. It's a totally foreign concept to him. So he laughs. He's still laughing when Niki calls to ask if he'll bring home some cough medicine.

He pulls the phone away from my desk, flipping the extension cord behind him to talk to her, to ask her why she needs it. (I know she can't shake off that cold—all spring she's looked like she has pneumonia or something, and I keep telling her to go see a doctor.)

Randy listens, standing in the doorway, his arm propped above his head, and I have to look away. But I can still see him in my mind, his wild blond hair catching the five o'clock sun through the doorway, his long body framed by that unreal and sleepy light.

I listen to him let her go through the old soft shoe of why she needs it. "Niki," he says, "if you can prove to me that you are really sick, and it isn't just from all those cigarettes you smoke, I'll buy you some medicine. Meantime, don't call me at work, okay?" He brings back the phone and struts off like he's some TV lawyer who's just scored brilliant points over a hardened criminal.

Niki never has any money of her own. Randy's too afraid she'll put something over on him. He likes to have total control, so he doles out money for groceries. Period. If she needs anything else, she actually has to beg. Then he wears her down with his questions and his logic. So she mostly gives up before she begins.

On Saturday afternoon, I go over to Niki's to baby-sit little Kristel. I never charge her anything. I just do it, once in a while. If she goes crazy, I don't want it to be on my conscience.

When I arrive at the apartment, Niki's all ready to go in tight, faded black jeans, high-heeled boots, and the fringed black leather jacket Randy gave her for Christmas. Her pale, skinny face is done up like some Albert Street hooker's. I never usually ask where she's going, but sometimes I give her money so she can go to a movie or buy lunch, whatever. I just shove a five- or ten-dollar bill in her pocket so she won't argue with me, and that's that.

I don't know if I'd rather see her like her usual self—

a bleached-out mouse—or like today. Her eyes are hard and glittery. She stabs out a cigarette in the avocado plant she's been nursing along, and she doesn't even bother to thank me for coming over. Or to kiss Kristel. Just breezes out the door with a flip of her scrawny hand. Her cowboy boots go thumpety-thumping down the echoey hall stairs before I get the door closed. I hadn't much cash to spare this week because I'm saving up for something. But I'd planned to at least slip her a couple of bucks.

It occurs to me that in spite of all my efforts, Niki may be cracking up, anyway. Why else would she go out looking like that—like she wants to get used by the first guy who says boo. Girls like Niki are everywhere. Somebody hurts them. They go out looking to be hurt again.

I would like to keep Kristel away from all that. I wish there was someplace you could lock kids up. Someplace safe like a two-acre park on top of a tremendously high building. With no elevators. You'd just lift them up on a big crane and let them off with their little lunch boxes. Several years later you could pick them up again, tall enough and tough enough to tell all the guys to take a flying leap off the edge of the world.

Kristel is going to be two next month. She's very alert to sudden noises; she looks at you with her bright brown eyes. "What's that?" she says, or "Oh, I hear a *ambliance*!" She's so smart, she speaks in full sentences. We play with a Fisher-Price village that Niki found at a Salvation Army thrift shop and bought with five dollars I gave her one

Saturday a couple of months ago. Most of the pieces are missing, but it still works.

Kristel makes the mail truck into the "ambliance." We have only three little plastic people. The black dentist becomes the doctor. The woman mail carrier is his nurse. The Fisher-Price family dog is "Baby," who has a bad cough—like Mummy. Kristel makes coughing sounds. Her socks are slipping off the ends of her toes. She puts Baby to bed on the edge of Randy and Niki's beat-up sofa. She lays her head on the cushion, closes her eyes, opens them, whips Baby off the sofa, and says, "All better now." She totters over, smiling, to show me. Her pale brown hair, almost the color Niki's used to be, is bunched up and matted at the back of her head. Her pajamas are stained with about two days' worth of ketchup. It's not like Niki to let her go dirty. She usually keeps her and everything else around this poor excuse for a home so clean you could eat off the top of the TV set.

I give Kristel a bath. When she is sweet-smelling again, like spring grass at Assiniboine Park after it's rained, I lay her down for a nap. She seems really happy I'm here and snuggles under her covers, still clutching the Fisher-Price dog, which I have to kiss before I kiss her.

The apartment is quiet, and everything has become filthy since I was here, only a week ago. I decide to do some cleaning because I hate sitting around with nothing to do. You start to remember things. That makes you nervous.

By around four-thirty, I've vacuumed, washed about a

dozen ashtrays, folded laundry, dusted, and scrubbed out the refrigerator, where, under the vegetable bin (containing half a head of rusty lettuce and a shrunken apple), some rotten meat and spilled milk have dripped together, congealed, and begun to stink up Niki's whole kitchen.

Kristel went off to lullaby land to the sound of the vacuum cleaner. The ring of the telephone startles her awake. She starts to whimper, so I lift her out of her crib. She snuggles into my neck as I carry her out to the living room and answer the phone on the fifth ring.

"Hi." Randy's sleepy voice comes at me like a sudden electric shock. My heart starts racing. "You baby-sitting again? Where's Niki?"

"She's out. She went out. She's shopping."

"Oh," he says.

There's this pause that seems to go on forever. I hear him breathing. Maybe looking out at whatever he's looking at with his hooded eyes.

"You're alone, then," he says.

"Yes, Randy, I'm alone. What the hell do you want?"

He laughs. "You sure are jumpy," he drawls.

"I'm busy," I say, leaning against the wall, sinking against the wall, with Kristel, his daughter, in my arms.

"You want me to come over?"

"No. I don't."

I slam down the phone, and my knees are shaking.

Not even ten minutes later, Niki gets home. She flops down at the kitchen table and says, "I've been saving some of that money you've been giving me."

"Oh?" I say, wondering what's coming next.

"Maybe," she says, watching me carefully, "just maybe I wouldn't have come back today."

"What do you mean?" I say, my mouth suddenly dry, my heart pounding. "You'd never leave Kristel."

"There's lots of things we'd never do. Swear we'd never do. We do them, though. Don't we, Rachel?"

Suddenly I feel sick. I've done this awful thing.

Niki says, looking me hard in the eyes with hers, so clear and sharp they feel like little knives peeling away my soul, "Rachel, I went to the bus station today. And I almost bought a ticket, you know? And can you guess where I was going?"

I have this terrible secret I've been keeping. A secret only Randy and I know about.

"Rachel, are you listening? I almost went to Boissevain. Twenty dollars one way. That's all it costs. I would have hitchhiked from there to the Peace Garden. Remember the summer we were twelve, and Grandpa drove us all that long way from Winnipeg? We camped over the weekend. Stayed at that lake—I forget the name."

"Lake William. In the Turtle Mountains."

"Yeah. That one. Well, that's where I was going."

Maybe she doesn't know. Maybe she hasn't guessed. I ask, "Do you remember how we caught those two fish and then we ate them?" This is a good memory. A safe memory. "Grandpa kept saying, 'This is the life! This is the way people should live! This is the real McCoy!' And then you burned your hand, and he told us stories until one in the morning so you wouldn't think about how much it hurt."

I watch her face. I wonder what she's thinking. Examining the back of her wrist, the tiny burn scar in the shape of a teardrop, she says, "*He* was the real McCoy, wasn't he? He never broke a promise."

"No, he never did."

"And you know what? Kristel has his eyes. They look right through you with so much love. They're wonderful, don't you think?"

I don't think I can trust my voice to speak.

"Kristel's the real McCoy, too, isn't she?"

"Yes." I take off my glasses. I rub my wet eyes and put the glasses on again. I love her. She's family. It all gets so confusing. It has to do with what we know and don't know about loving. It has to do with how we each have to learn the right way to love and not be always taken in by the kind of guys who'll disappoint us over and over again.

"I wouldn't really have gone, Rachel. I swear it. I wouldn't really have done that. It was just," she says, "that I finally decided I wanted—that I *had to*—feel better."

Her cheeks are pink, and her eyes are finally soft with the kind of sadness that isn't hard to look at. It's her old inside gleam that I thought I might never see again.

If I told her about Randy and me, it would make her realize, all the more, that she has to leave him. But I can't do that. I have to keep promising myself that I will never never tell her about that. And I will personally kill Randy if he ever so much as hints at it to her. It would be the end of everything for Niki and me. And what would that prove? Who would help her then?

"Niki, I swear, you're going to make it." I fold her into my arms and hold her tight. "I just know you're going to. And I'm going to keep right on helping you. I'm going to do all that I can."

"I know that," she says, clinging to me, her voice hoarse like she's about to break apart inside. "I know you will. You've always been such a good friend to me."

Traveling On into the Light ✢ ✢ ✢ ✢

Several months after my father left us, I got a letter. I knew he had relocated to Santa Fe, but that was it. Whenever he'd call, I'd tell Mom to tell him I didn't want to talk to him. Anyway, in the letter he asked, if he sent the ticket, would I fly south and visit him. And his "new friend."

My dad's an art dealer. He'd met this guy on one of his buying trips. "And," said my mother, who could barely speak for pain, "fell in love with him."

Dad and I had always been close. My mom and I hadn't. So it came as a total surprise to me that he should abandon her for this "other life." Why couldn't he have been as honest with me as I have always been with him? *That* was the cruelest hurt of all.

So I talked to my friend Rod, who is gay, too. "Oh,

come on, Sam!" He kind of reeled back in his chair. "What'd you expect? A kiss-and-tell confession to his *daughter*? You couldn't have handled it."

Mom said, "Take the trip."

"Mom," I said, shocked, "how can you say that after what he's done to you?"

"Sammy," she replied, "you are sixteen years old. There are so many things you don't know about life yet that my reasons for telling you to go would take days to explain."

This was one of the reasons Mom and I had never gotten along.

"Don't be angry with me, honey," she said, taking my hand. We were driving down Portage Avenue in the middle of downtown traffic. "Just go and find out for yourself. If you don't, you'll always regret it."

When I got off Mesa Airlines at Santa Fe, I was met by Dad and *this person*—to whom I took an instant dislike. It was a hot July day. He wore a heavy turquoise necklace and a brown leather shirt that looked expensive. Like a gift. My father's gift.

Freeloader. That was my instant assessment. Older men often leave their wives for younger money-grubbing women. Here was my father doing the same thing, more or less, with a guy who couldn't have been more than five or six years older than me.

"This is Bernardo Yellowhorse. Everyone calls him Nardo." My father practically caressed the name.

"Hello . . . Bernardo." I froze him with a smile.

"Hi, Sam." He faded back into a patch of sunlight so brilliant it almost made him disappear.

"Well," said Dad. "How is your mother?"

"She'll live," I said, with arrow perfection.

He winced and, hand on my back, steered me off to the car.

He didn't ask about Mom again until we were on our way. "We're about ten miles out of town." He tapped his fingers on the steering wheel. "Those are the Sangre de Cristo Mountains you see in the distance," he said, glancing out across the baked landscape at a low ridge of blue. "Is your mom planning to stay at the house?"

"Why don't you ask her yourself?"

"I already have. She wasn't sure, last time I talked to her. I said if she needed anything, to give me a call."

"Really."

"Really."

Bernardo shifted in the backseat. I am tall, but he's about six-foot-four, and I had jammed my seat back as far as it would go. It gave me considerable pleasure to know that his legs were likely screaming with pain.

When it seemed that I wasn't going to give up any more details, Dad said, "I hope you brought along some warm clothes. Santa Fe is about a mile above sea level, so even though you are now in sunny New Mexico, the evenings get kind of cool."

A car whizzed past us with a yellow license plate that read NEW MEXICO—LAND OF ENCHANTMENT.

"Santa Fe is the oldest state capital in the Union," Dad said, playing the role of affable tour guide. "It's

Old World Spanish. Founded in 1612. Nardo," he said, leaning toward the backseat, "I think we'll drop by the gallery first."

"Fine," said Bernardo. "I need to get back to work."

"Nardo has a studio at the back of the gallery," said Dad with pride (I didn't know for which: his art gallery or Bernardo). "He's a real up-and-comer. Only one year since he graduated from the Institute of American Indian Arts, and already he's cracking a real tough nut—the Santa Fe art scene. We have buyers from all over the world making offers on his work."

"Terrific," I said, poking my fingernail into the soft gray leather of my father's BMW.

So maybe old Nardo wasn't a freeloader. In my eyes, however, he still seemed a ridiculous mate for my father. Right then I made up my mind to tell him so, and at the first opportunity.

The gallery, in the center of town, was on a street called Galisteo. As we got closer, I could see that everything was as my father had said: very Spanish—the streets were narrow, with wrought-iron gates leading to inner courtyards or tree-lined back lanes. A lot of the window frames and doorways were painted sky blue, and, against the reddish clay of adobe walls, hollyhocks and roses grew up in a strangely beautiful partnership.

I rolled down my window, and the smell of this new world was different, too, a faint but pungently smoky perfume.

"Piñon fires," said Dad, picking up on this. "That's what everyone burns around here. The piñon pine cone

also contains those little nuts that you and I were so fond
of buying, back in Winnipeg, on our Saturday mornings
at DeLuca's."

Of course he had to bring that up. Reminding me of
how he'd been such a swell father. I hated the way I was
feeling. I'd planned to at least handle all of this with
maturity. But parents can really bring out the worst in a
person, with their expectations and subtle little guilt
trips.

We parked in front of the Sandoval Gallery. With
a quick look at Dad, I said, "I thought this was *your*
gallery."

"It is," he said. "But I'm in partnership with Luis
Sandoval."

"How come it doesn't have your name, too?"

He laughed, opening my door, and said, "Because he
was here first."

Bernardo untangled his limbs and made it past the
gallery's heavy front doors right on through to his studio
before Dad and I had even stepped inside.

The gallery was cool and carpeted, with Native American art on the walls, on Plexiglas pedestals, and in glass
cases. My eye went to a small turquoise frog with red
eyes.

"That's a Zuni fetish," said a slim young woman behind
the glass counter. She wore a long flowing skirt with a
silver belt. Her hair was pulled back into a high, loose
bun. Silver and coral dangled from her ears, and around
her neck, on a thin leather thong, hung a pewter amulet,
an odd little stick figure with a hunchback who played

what looked like a flute. "He's an Anasazi spirit," she said, looking down at where my eyes had landed. "His name is Kokopelli."

"Janine, this is my daughter," said Dad.

"Hello, Sam." She extended a gentle hand and shook mine.

"Janine keeps this place rolling," Dad said with a smile. "When the rest of us are a little strung out, she always manages to bring things back to some sort of state of grace. We call her the Mediator."

I smiled at Janine. I liked her.

"If you have some things to do, Stuart," she said, coming around the counter, "I'll show her around."

"Sam admires beauty," said Dad, and paused, about to say something else.

Beauty was a thing he and I had always agreed on. One of the favorite lines from one of our favorite songs, a song he used to sing to me, was "You are too beautiful, my dear, to be true, and I am a fool for beauty."

Janine folded her hands and smiled. At the rug. There were tears in my father's eyes. I looked away, too, and felt a sharp pang over my heart. Why did he have to bring this up? I felt like I'd been standing on a stool and he'd just come along and kicked out the legs from under me.

"Well," Dad said, recovering himself. "Have you heard from Luis?"

"He called not more than five minutes ago, asking the same thing about you," said Janine. "He got held up. He'll be here soon."

She tucked her cool fingers under my elbow. "Bernardo's work is very beautiful," she said. "Did your father tell you that Nardo is Luis's nephew?"

"His *nephew?*" I stammered.

I watched my father's back disappear up the carpeted stairs to a glassed-in loft, and then it hit me: I'd totally jumped the gun on Bernardo. He wasn't Dad's lover at all. It was Luis, Dad's partner. The one I hadn't met yet.

I wished for a strong wind to come along and blow my ashes out to the canyons and mesas I'd seen from the plane window. But Janine was already guiding me through to the back.

Flute music, recorded with a background of ocean waves washing onto a shore, drifted through Nardo's high-ceilinged studio. Pink-tinged sunlight slipped past green leaves beyond the windows, and three slanted skylights framed patches of blue.

He'd changed into jeans and an old T-shirt. Bent in concentration over a light table, he still wore the heavy necklace—but now, on his own turf, it didn't seem so out of place.

"He's working on a new collection," said Janine. "He's calling it 'Traveling On into the Light.' Nardo," she said quietly to his back, "I know Sam would like to see the piece you've just finished."

I would have felt better if he'd chosen to be as rude to me as I'd been to him. But he turned and smiled, teeth unbelievably white, and said, "Sure. It's over here."

My God, I thought, he's beautiful. How could I have

missed this? "This is really really very very nice of you," I babbled idiotically.

"No problem," he said with a small smile.

It was a large canvas. The left third held a towering cliff. Rising over it was a crescent moon in a dark sky and stars painted like four-pointed crosses. It was winter. At the base of the cliff sat an old woman, wrapped in a blanket, holding a small exquisite bowl. Four perfect kernels of corn, sitting petal-like on the bottom, were all it contained. The eyes in her strong face looked beyond snow to where the canvas slowly began to shift to the dry heat of summer and, it seemed, to another century.

There, the sun slanted on a young woman with long black hair, dressed in jeans and a white T-shirt. She walked along the edge of a green pond, a dragonfly perched on her shoulder. A second dragonfly flew above her head. Another followed, floating near her feet. A fourth fluttered on ahead.

The wonder of these morning dragonflies was that they mirrored the cross-shaped stars on the nighttime side of the painting.

I felt dazzled, and slightly dizzy. I didn't know whether to smile or cry or laugh or scream. Finally, I said, "I've got to tell you, this is one of the most confusing days of my life."

Nardo did the strangest thing. He reached out and fingered a piece of my hair, lifting it, examining it as if he'd never seen anything like it.

"Can you see this?" he asked me.

I had long straight hair like the young woman in his

painting, so the piece he held was far enough away from my face that I could see it. And I thought that that's what he meant: literally—could I see it?

I said, "Yes," with a nervous laugh.

He smiled, still looking at my hair, and it was then I noticed that Janine was no longer in the room.

"It's black as a raven's wing," he said. "But the sunlight changes it. And I'll bet the moonlight does, too."

I felt shy when he talked about the moonlight. I noticed he did, too, because he let the strand drop. He quickly perched himself on the edge of a worktable.

"You've got to learn something about shadow and light," he told me, looking at his feet, gently swinging them back and forth. "My grandfather used to say: 'The eyes play tricks. And the mind often lies. It's the heart that's the true way.' "

I sighed and shyly edged up beside him, my arms folded. "Your grandfather must have been a magician. He talked in riddles."

"Nobody can tell you what to do," he said in a soft voice, looking sidelong at me. "All I can say is it's okay to feel confused in your head. But that's not the place where you're going to recognize the truth."

I could tell you now about how Dad looked, all nervous and expectant, when he and Luis walked through the studio door. I could tell you that Luis, a tall, striking man with gray-streaked hair, walked right up to me and put his arms around me and hugged me for quite a while. I could also tell you that I was a brat for the next two weeks and didn't give Dad two words, but Luis and I got on like crazy. He plays the French horn, and so do I. We found some old sheet music and played duets and woke up the neighbors. The night before I left, he took me out for dinner, and at the end of it, over Frozen Chocolate Mud Pie, he looked across the table at me, frowned behind his wire-rims, and sighed. "Samantha, if you don't make up with your father, I'm going to smack you. I mean it."

But what I really want to tell you is, when Dad and I finally did make up, it wasn't in some dramatic moment. It was quite small, really. It happened the next summer toward the end of my second visit to Santa Fe.

It was about eight o'clock at night, and I just happened to walk in as Dad and Luis had their heads bent, in unison, examining something on a light table. It was dark in the studio, so that just their faces were lit up— lit by the soft, reflected light. They looked, somehow, so right together, the way good couples do. And I was struck, all of a sudden, by my father's courage. There is no other word for it.

Moonlight Sonata ✝ ✝ ✝ ✝

For Tim, Kate, Susan, and my adopted son, Jack Clarke

I was ten years old when my father committed suicide. He bought a shotgun secondhand off a guy he knew. Then he drove, alone, to our cottage on Cormorant Lake and blew his brains out. It was Thanksgiving weekend. My mother had prepared a turkey with a different kind of stuffing—she put oysters in it—and roasted it on the barbecue. I remember things like that. I have been told I have a good eye for detail.

Anyway, we never went to the cottage after that. My mother sold it. She found a real estate agent named Joe Harris, who had a fondness for widows—my mother included. I understand all this now, because Joe still shows up once in a while. At the time, though, I thought he was just being kind. You learn things about human beings as you grow older that you'd just as soon not know.

They say there was blood all over the walls and the curtains and the windows and the old piano near where they found him. He'd been playing that piano, likely, just before he did it, because he blew himself right off the bench. I know what he was playing, too. It was the *Moonlight* Sonata. How I know is it was one of his favorites and probably the only piece he ever played well.

His leave-taking was planned. He left specific instructions, giving me, a ten-year-old kid, his truck and a beaded smoky-smelling moose-hide jacket I'd always admired and which had hung in plastic in his closet ever since I could remember.

My father wasn't a man who liked killing things. Other kids' dads would go out to the country during duck or goose hunting season, but he never did. I went only once, with my friend Scott and his dad, Bart.

It was the year after Dad died. I remember Bart running down their back porch steps with a box of shells and his gun, hollering, "Get your arses into that car." And Scotty grinning at me as we shoved and tripped each other, trying to see who could get into the backseat first. But in the marsh, as the sun went down and the wind came up, it got cold sitting in the canoe. In between long periods of boredom, Bart lifted his gun and blasted away. Ducks honked wildly, black against the reddening sky, and he shot as many as he could. Some still alive, some stone dead, they hurtled into the water. A few flapped away into the reeds; Scotty and I heard them in there, splashing around, lost and forgotten, calling out in an awful way.

The ducks floating nearby, the ones Bart did eventually pick up, he tied together by their necks in a strange bouquet. He threw them in the trunk, and on the way home, we could smell them. Now, years later, I still remember that smell.

Suicide is not something you get over quickly. Maybe even never. It's turned my mother, who used to be happy all the time, into a quiet, nervous woman. She smokes too much. She wears tight pants. I can't remember the last time I saw her in a dress. Her lips and her eyes, which used to have a soft, open look like she was in the continuous glow of some daydream, are hard now. In the winter, her skin draws across her bones like the head of some dead animal left out on the prairies to dry.

Just the other day, I told Scott, "I keep watching her face for something in it to *happen*, know what I mean?"

"*Typical,*" he said, disgusted. "Listen, we've been friends a long time, right? And I gotta tell you something, Jamie. Out of every bad thing happening, some good comes. Like your old man blowing his brains out and leaving you a truck. Now that's what I call thoughtful. Wish my old man would kick off." He torqued me a beer.

"No, thanks," I said. "I'm not drinking anymore, remember?"

"Right." He tossed back the beer and plugged on it himself. Lowering the bottle, he picked away at the label, belched. "You're no fun anymore."

"Great. Seven months ago, I'm trashed out of my head all the time and you call me a drooling fool. Now that I'm sober, you tell me I'm no fun. Don't be an asshole."

"Now that's more like it." Scott squinted one eye, lifting his finger from the beer bottle and pointing it at me.

"What."

"You're testy, man. You're finally saying what's on your mind."

"I can't say anything to Gretchen. Nothing."

"So ditch the bitch."

"I beg your pardon?"

"Oh, sorry. I forgot she's your flower, or something. Jeez, Sinclair, you're such a poet." He fell over, cackling.

A girl I knew, last year, told me I reminded her of Jim Morrison. "You're dangerous," she said. "And you're almost always alone, and every girl I know thinks you secretly write poetry, and they all wish it was for them."

It's been a rough year for me. It's one thing to look dangerous and poetic and lonely and on the edge, and quite another to actually live it. Scott got tired of it after a while and started to make excuses not to be with me.

I finally woke up one cold morning this past March, sitting in the truck in the dark, musty garage, and I didn't remember how I got there. I decided, even if it meant ruining my reputation, that this was a really tiresome and deeply stupid way to live.

I also decided that I'd never actually liked the taste of booze. And just thinking about it, with the smell of puke, in my dad's hand-me-down, father-to-son truck, was enough to make me want to toss up again.

There was a little crack down the window on the driver's side, and blood in my hair. My head healed. I'd somehow managed to save up some money from my part-time job pumping gas at Petro-Can, so I had the window replaced, and at the same time put in a tape deck. It was right about that time, too, that I joined AA, Scott and I started being friends again, and I noticed Marina Elaine Gretchen Hendricks for the first time.

She's never been one to be easily won over. I could tell that when I first saw her, tall and beautiful and serious, a lone flower among a lot of thorns, in the hall-way at school. I watched her for an entire month before I made my first move. Discovered all I could about her. Asked around. She liked foreign films and the ballet, somebody said. I watched her in class doodle carnations all over her purple binder. Later, I found out that she hated purple. I noted the Greenpeace and Save the Earth buttons she wore on her sweaters—three sweaters, all Icelandic wool, in natural colors. And she always wore black under the sweaters: black jeans, black tights, black skirts.

Once, she wore a T-shirt to school that said QUESTION REALITY. The next week, five other girls bought the same shirt. I overheard her tell somebody in the hall that she was never going to wear that shirt again. At this point, I finally felt that I had enough information to get her to notice me. At noon that same day, I sauntered into the cafeteria, whistling "Strawberry Fields Forever," and gently elbowed several people out of the way to get in line behind her.

As she reached for an egg salad sandwich, I said, "I'm glad you decided against the tuna fish."

She swiftly turned, blond braid swinging down her back, to look at who'd said that.

"Did you read," I said, looking into her incredibly sexy eyes, "about all those dolphins that are dying because they get caught in the nets along with the tuna?"

"I won't ever touch tuna fish again," she said, her nostrils flaring. "You don't eat it, do you?"

"Absolutely not," I replied with sincere conviction. "I've given it up." I said this even though I've never touched the stuff.

Gretchen, the only woman in the world who could make me believe that there really is a kind, just, and all-seeing God, puts up with my moods. I'm hoping that she'll also eventually sleep with me. Coming up, though, is our Platonic Thanksgiving Weekend. Which is fine just so long as I can have her with me.

I told Scott about Thanksgiving (a holiday that has given my mother and me a deep hatred for turkey), but just the part about Gretchen coming camping with me.

"Now *there's* a move in the right direction," Scotty said with a leer. "So where are you guys going?"

I didn't exactly say. I fudged around a bit. Scott, like Gretchen, is selective about what he figures I should be thinking.

"I guess I could tell Mom that I'm spending the weekend with Sally James and her kid brother and their crazy hippie parents," Gretchen said when I asked her. "She always believes me. She'll never know the difference unless somebody tells her—which they won't. But why Cormorant Lake? What's there?"

"Just a little town and a resort area," I said vaguely. "I've been there before. It's pretty. Lots of trees."

"When?"

"When, what?"

"Were you there?"

"A long time ago—I forget."

"You forget?"

"I need to get away and think about things, okay?"

"That's why you want me to go? To help you think about things?"

"I just want you to come with me. Do I have to go into deep psychological explanations?"

We were parked in front of her house. I try never to meet up with her mother, who carries a briefcase and wears suits and heavy gold jewelry.

Gretchen held my eyes with hers until I started to worry that she knew I was giving her selective information. Finally she said, "I have to be back to watch Mom and Dad and my sisters and aunts and uncles and cousins eat the turkey—which is all they really care about as far as this weekend is concerned, anyway. But I have got to be back *here*, *then*, Jamie. I absolutely have to."

Why my father would leave a ten-year-old a reasonably new, mint-condition Chevy pickup (he'd bought it for odd jobs, like hauling wood, around the cottage) is something I've never been able to figure out. Until my sixteenth birthday, a year ago, it just sat first in our old garage and then at our new place.

Over the years, I figure I must have, in total, spent at

least a couple of months' worth of hours in the garage, sitting inside the truck, waiting until I was old enough to get my driver's license.

One Saturday, when I was around fourteen years old, I felt so sagged out with looking in the glove compartment and always finding the same old yellow plastic window scraper and the same old black comb and the bill from some restaurant, all ragged at the corners and still totaling $6.42 every single frigging time I looked at it, that I went on a major hunting rampage. I pulled out the seat. I pulled up the floor mats. I ran my fingers along every available inch of goddamn plastic and chrome. What I came up with was a single rusty beer-bottle cap, probably left there by me, a dusty drinking straw (same source), a small screw, and a pamphlet issued by Ducks Unlimited. I stared at that pamphlet for a long time. I read it over and over. It didn't tell me anything that I wanted to know. I twisted it up, lit a match to it, and held it outside the window until it burned my fingers so I had to let it drop.

The next day, Sunday, I pulled Dad's beaded moose-hide jacket from the back of my closet. (I keep it in its original plastic bag to seal in the smoky smell of the tanned hide). This time, it almost fit. Wearing it, I went and sat in the truck. I stayed there all day, with the windows closed, staring out the windshield at the garage wall.

Around suppertime, Mom surprised me by cranking open the door on the passenger's side. She just stared at me for a minute. She has large eyes in a small face, and her hair always hangs over her eyebrows. She climbed up inside and closed the door.

Leaning her head back, she closed her eyes. Then she opened them wide and looked at me and said, "Life goes by too goddamn fast, don't you think?"

"Yes," I said, even though for me it never went by fast enough.

She reached up her hand, then, and lightly tucked my hair behind my ear, something she'd done when I was smaller just before she kissed me good-night.

"You're thinking about your dad, aren't you?"

"Yes," I said, and this time she was right.

She smoothed her fingers along the front of Dad's jacket, then laid her head back on the seat again. "I am so sorry," she said, "about this life we're leading." She looked at me again. "I wish it were different. I wish I could change it."

"At the lake," I said, "what did he do besides play the piano?"

"Wandered off. God knows where."

"You don't know where?"

"He'd go down along the beach, then he'd keep right on walking until he disappeared. I think maybe he walked off up into the hills."

"You never went with him?"

"I thought it was what he wanted. He always seemed to need more space than I could give him."

"But why did he do it? Why did he kill himself?"

"I don't know, honey. Maybe he figured he didn't belong anywhere in this world. And I guess he was depressed. Depression does terrible things to people."

"You're not depressed, are you, Mom?"

She swallowed and stared hard ahead. "I'm okay," she said.

It's five o'frigid clock on this quiet Friday, and I'm parked in the truck two blocks down and across the street from Gretchen's, and here she appears in my rearview mirror looking like some Madonna in a back alley dream—skintight black jeans, blond hair in a single braid, her weekend possessions in a bulging blue duffel bag tucked under her fat-sweatered arm, the thick watch that I gave her flopping down her skinny wrist.

I reach over, flip the handle of the truck-cab door, which flies open in a sudden gust of wind. Gretchen swings up inside, kicks her duffel bag against the heater, and struggles with the wind for possession of the door.

"Scott is real mad at you," she says, finally banging it shut. With her small hand, she smooths a wisp of silky hair back into her braid. "He says for you to drop dead and go straight to hell."

"Love him, too," I say, wheeling away from the curb.

"He's *serious*." She props her foot sideways on the dash and leans on her elbow against the window. Tom Petty & the Heartbreakers are just getting into "Runnin' Down a Dream." "He says you've got to forget your dad's suicide. And he says you've tricked me into encouraging you to wallow all over yourself."

"What? I don't know what you're talking about," I say, planning to knock Scotty's block off the next time I see him.

"Jamie"—she reaches over, flicks off the tape—"why didn't you tell me Cormorant Lake is the place where your dad committed suicide? Why did you lie to me?"

"I didn't think you'd come with me."

"You're absolutely right. I wouldn't have. Scott says it isn't going to do you any good, and I agree with him. In fact, it'll probably make matters worse. It'll dredge up all that awful stuff all over again. And you've got to start forgetting about it."

"Terrific," I say, inching down the window. "I'm surrounded by psychiatrists."

I take a couple of deep breaths of cold, smoky autumn air. We live close to the edge of the city. Farmers are burning stubble in the surrounding countryside. Thanksgiving bonfires. Their smoke is a memory. I've always liked it.

I roll up the window again so that Gretchen won't get cold. We drive past a Mr. Submarine, a gas station, a Canada Tire store, some bushes, and a little farmhouse that faces the city and backs onto a bald patch of land that isn't yet given over to progress. Soon, there are highway signs telling us we can roll along at ninety klicks, then a bridge over a river, then a truck stop, which we pass going ninety-five.

Gretchen pouts against the door. I reach under my legs, pull out a bag of jelly doughnuts—her favorites—and put them on the seat between us. She looks out the window. I make crinkling sounds with the bag, opening it her way so that the luscious smell of sugar and grease wafts up her perfect nostrils.

As I said, she's never been one to be easily won over. Minutes pass. We get up to the highway sign that says REDWELL, 3 KM. We drive past the Redwell exit. Finally, near Pine Bluff, she steals her hand into the doughnut bag and pulls one out. She bites into it in an uninterested manner; her lips still pout as she chews.

"There's sugar on your chin," I say, and I start to hum a little tune as we go along down the highway on this gray hour before the setting of the sun.

It's about a two-hour drive out to the lake. The year before the suicide, I was allowed to bring a friend out to the cottage with me just about every weekend. I chose Scott. To pass the time in the car, Mom encouraged us to play Geography. It wasn't so bad, except a lot of places end in *a*'s or *o*'s, and if you're nine years old, you soon run out of places that start with those letters.

"Want to play Geography?" I ask Gretchen.

She licks red jelly off the corner of her mouth, rattles the bag for another doughnut. Sugar always puts her in a better mood.

"Sure," she says in a neutral voice.

"Know how to play?"

"No."

"I say Alberta. Then you say Algiers. Then I say Siberia, and you say Antarctica."

"And you say Antwerp," she says.

"Very good. Pelican Rapids."

"Pelican Rapids?"

"Yeah. Pelican Rapids. It's an Indian reservation, up north. I think. Next would be . . . Selkirk."

"I don't know any *K*'s."

"Sure you do—think. It's one of the things you do best."

"And what's that supposed to mean?"

I grin at her to show I'm just a swell guy in a super-happy mood.

"Kamloops." She sighs, and rolls her head back on the seat.

"See? It's easy. San Francisco."

"It's boring. Ontario."

"Can you think of something better to do?" I reach over, clasp her knee, and say slowly, "Oslo."

She pulls away and says, "I spy with my little eye."

"What?"

"A boy who needs his head examined." She drops her half-eaten doughnut, oozing jelly, back into the bag, turns away again to her window, tucks her hands up inside her sleeves, and pretends to go to sleep.

Rubbing my hands along the steering wheel, feeling the bumps, I say to myself, She's here, isn't she. And that's the best luck in the world, even if I am a selfish shit-head for lying to her about where we're going.

Pretty soon she's breathing softly, and I can tell that she's actually fallen asleep and that I don't have to worry about her going anywhere. She's right here beside me, where I can look at her. Gretchen, asleep, is the most beautiful sight in the world.

Sometimes little things like being able to watch some-body you care about doing something simple, like just sleep, make you so happy that if you weren't careful, you could end up driving down the highway bawling like a baby.

Out in the fields, the fires running along the rows of piled-up stubble are bright and kind of eerie. I turn the heater on low. It's too cold to sleep outside. Camping is a dumb idea. She won't agree to a motel—which neither of us could afford, anyway. It's going to get cramped in this truck, and what if her parents find out she spent the weekend with me? They aren't exactly what you'd call enthused about their daughter dating a recovering alco-holic, if you get my meaning, so the *merde* would hit the fan in a major way. They might try to stop her from seeing me again, and if I couldn't see Gretchen anymore, I'd just as soon buy a shotgun and blow my own head off.

The thing about the cold prairie sun going down is that you start to imagine awful stuff, and you could lose it if you didn't tell yourself to stop thinking that way.

Whenever things get bad, no kidding, first place I think about is the lake—even though I haven't been there for seven years. I think about the white gulls that fly around and over all the small docks and the beaches and the smell of washed-up dried cattails, and I think about toasting marshmallows under the moon and Mom calling me to come to bed and Dad at the piano when I'd finally come in and how he'd look away from the keys, a drink on the ledge by the bottom keys, and say, "C'mere, son," and I'd go to him and he'd put his big arm around me and pull me close and that was the only time in my memory that I can recall him hugging me. Just those times at the lake.

Sometimes, now, when I hold Gretchen, I feel happy, the way Dad seemed to be when he was at the lake. But then I start to see blood on the cottage walls. The blood I never got to see but only heard about. Then I have to hold her closer to block it out. I have to smell her perfume and talk nonsense in her ear and feel her warm body all against me in order to stop my father's blood from coming sneaking up behind my closed eyes.

I want to tell Gretchen how I feel about her. But I never do. I don't tell her how much I love her, or even *that* I love her. She already has too much power over me, so it just stays a secret locked up inside me.

She shifts in her seat and turns her sleeping face toward me. With a little murmur, she suddenly wakes up and catches me looking at her.

"Where are we?" she says, stretching.

"About a half hour out of the city," I tell her, reaching out to turn down the heat. The little lever is stiff, and you've always got to give it a good yank.

"Oh," she says, still looking at me. Her eyes are dark blue. One of them has a hazel-colored V that kind of glances down the far right side of her iris. "How long does it take to get there?"

"About another hour and a half," I say, looking away, because Gretchen's eyes could almost make you drive off the road.

"It'll be dark when we get there, then," she says. "How

will we see in the dark?" She adds, answering herself, "We'll have to build a fire on the beach. Good thing I brought a candle."

"The wind will blow out your candle," I say with a laugh.

She goes sullen on me again. Though she's probably smarter than me, she gets insecure when you call her attention to things.

"The moon will be out. We won't need candles," I say lightly.

"I don't see it. Where is it? Where is the moon?"

"It'll be out—keep your shirt on." I reach over and stroke my hand along the back of her neck under her braid. "There'll be a full bright moon that you could practically read by."

"Good," she breathes, relaxing. "It'd better be a big one."

We hold hands until she doesn't want to anymore. She pulls away and huddles in her corner of the seat.

The road that turns off to Viceroy Beach, where the cottage is, runs through a small town that has seen better days. The one thing that's kept the town going is the beach population. But Cormorant Lake has been in the paper for the past two summers because of the newsworthy levels of *E. coli* bacteria from all the human waste that's been dumped into it every year since God knows when. It's also drying up like a lot of other lakes. I'll bet that's because of the hole in the ozone layer and the selfishness, basically, of the human race—myself included. If I were conscientious, I'd sell my truck and walk everywhere.

Around twenty after seven, just over two hours since leaving the city limits, we roll over the railroad tracks that transect the main drag of town. There's a truck and a red Fiat parked in front of the building that used to be a café and that's now called Brenda's Lakeside Inn, subtitled: Coffee Shop, Groceries, Take-Out Food, Bag Ice, Movie Rentals. The wood trim that was once painted dark green has been freshly painted white.

I nudge Gretchen awake. "Want to stop in for a coffee or something?"

We're both caffeine addicts. It's one thing we've always agreed on.

Brenda, or maybe it's her daughter, sleepily serves us and brings Gretchen, along with the coffee, a small order of fries on a big plate.

"I bet these have been microwaved." Gretchen holds one up, and it limply bends in half. She picks up a ketchup bottle, and I laugh as she does this maniac shake to get about two drops onto her plate. She swirls one of the rubbery fries in the ketchup, pops it into her mouth. She picks up another and slowly drags it around the plate, making pale red ketchup lines.

"Where are we going to sleep tonight?" she says, without looking up.

"In the truck?" I suggest hopefully.

"The *truck*?"

"I dunno. Where should we sleep?"

"I guess—the truck." She squishes her fry into her plate like the butt end of a cigarette.

I reach out and take hold of her hand. She tries to pull away, but I keep holding on. "I'm really sorry about all this," I say lamely.

"Sorry?" She smiles sarcastically. "Why be sorry? I'm having a terrific time. Sophisticated surroundings. Gourmet fries."

"You want to go back?" I know she'll say no, so there's no harm in asking.

She sighs heavily. "Please stop twisting me around, and tell me what you're planning to do. Peer in the windows of your old cottage—or what?"

"Something like that." I give her a smile I don't feel and add, "Doo-doo. Doo-doo. Doo-doo-doo-doo-doo-doo," like in the movie *Jaws*.

She pulls away. "You'll look at . . . *it*, the cottage, tomorrow. Okay? Then I want to go home."

"Okay."

"You won't look at it until tomorrow? Promise me."

"Right. But we'll go down and stay at the beach tonight, okay?"

Even though the idea scares me, I want to see the cottage in the moonlight. I want to walk along the beach and get sand in my socks, build a fire, toast a few marshmallows, and, when I've got up enough nerve, go stand on the deck and look in the living room windows.

I wonder if the people who own it now will be around this weekend. When we were there, people usually closed up their places on the September long weekend.

As we're leaving Brenda's, I pick up a bag of stale marshmallows from a shelf by the door, throw her some extra money, and tell her to keep the change. My part-time job at Petro-Can allows me to be generous sometimes.

We head off with the truck's beams on low. A few swaying trees are bare of leaves; others have completely turned color. Against the tall grasses along the ditch, an old paper bag is crouched down in the wind like a cat waiting for its prey.

In wet summers, I remember, the narrow, incredibly steep gravel road everybody took down to Viceroy Beach would sometimes get so soft that by the end of the weekend, it would be deeply rutted. I used to imagine that what we left behind us was silence. Just that and our tracks.

Gearing down into second, we turn a corner, and below us a crater-etched moon, big as a house, gleams on the water.

"Look at that big moon! Didn't I promise you? See? I hung it just for you. Right over the lake."

We crawl toward it. Gretchen's clutching the armrest, her right foot pressed against an imaginary brake pedal. I roll down the window, lean out, and listen to the crunch of gravel. The wet smell of fall and mulching leaves is in the air.

"It's really beautiful here," I say, bringing in my head.

"Jesus, Jamie," she says, looking over the dashboard as the road continues to bump and wind away beneath us.

I park the truck at the edge of the beach, making

it parallel to the lake so that we can see the awesome moon and the small farms and communities at the other side, where lights, here and there, are strung out like a connect-the-dots illustration.

"So," says Gretchen. "This is it."

"Yep."

Her hand is on the door handle. "Are we getting out, or what?"

"Sure." I flip open my door and jump down from the cab. The dark sand is unexpectedly soft, and, hands shoved in my jeans pockets, I trip around in it before walking over to the lake. The bright water, catching the moon, rushes ghostly cascades into shore.

Gretchen comes up behind me. I turn. She looks small, shivering in her big sweater. "It's lonely here," she says in a low voice.

"Just the time of year, I guess."

She comes right up and leans against me with a big, sad sigh. I unzip my jacket and steer her around in front of me. Then I wrap her, back against me, inside the jacket and start to do up the zipper. She giggles. I carefully zip it up as far as it'll go with her inside, almost to her neck. I hold her tight and sway her back and forth and kiss her hair. Gretchen's hair is soft as a cloud. I feel happier than I've felt since I can't remember when.

"You were right, sort of." She awkwardly tries to look up at me.

"About what?" I murmur thickly, because her hair, in fact everything about her, drives me crazy.

"About the moon, Jamie." She pulls her head away. "The *moon*."

"Right. Oh, yeah. The moon. Do you want to fool around?"

"God," she says, squirming inside my jacket. "Is that all you ever think about?"

"Yep. I have to think about it. For us both. Right?"

She stomps on my sneaker with hers. I painfully unzip my jacket and set her free.

"How come you don't like me?" I say, just kidding around—but not really. I watch her bend down and pick up an old beer-bottle cap, a remnant from some summer beach party.

"How come you don't like *me*?" she snaps back.

"I like you," I say, surprised.

"No, you don't." She tosses the cap away. "You don't respect me. You manipulate me. I'm just a convenience to you."

"A what? Beg your pardon?"

"And your strong-and-silent routine makes me feel lonelier than you can ever imagine." She walks back to the truck, yanks on the passenger door. It's always hard to open. "Dammit, dammit, dammit." She goes around and kicks the front tire.

"*Don't do that!* Okay?"

She heaves an enormous sigh that practically shakes her off her feet. "God," she says.

"Gretchen?" I walk up to her. "I don't know what you expect. Sure, I clam up about stuff. But I'm still thinking. . . . I think all the time."

She gives me an angry, hurt look. "Nobody said you were stupid, Jamie. The problem is you think too much."

She looks off down the lake. "You going to build a fire or something? I'm cold." She hugs herself. "And it *is* dark. I don't care what you say about the moon."

I get the flashlight from the truck, then go around the beach and back into the bushes looking for dry twigs and fallen branches. While I'm doing this, Gretchen huddles against the truck because she's too proud or stubborn or cold to go around to the driver's side and get in. It takes a bit of doing and a book and a half of matches (I burn my goddamn thumb) to get a fire going, but I'm supposed to be the strong one here, providing warmth and protection, or whatever, so that nothing happens to her.

The flames finally lick, then blaze, then crackle. I encourage her to come and sit with me in front of the fire. I've built it inside a ring of stones that somebody else left from a previous time. I'm hoping she'll notice— think I've gathered stones myself, for her benefit. But she just sits, hugging her knees. She won't talk to me and I don't know what to do.

After about five minutes of nothing from her, I finally get up and say, "I'm going down the beach, okay? Stay here. You'll be fine, and I won't be long. Okay, Gretchen? It's a big fire."

I start to walk away. I can't stand it when she doesn't talk to me. It makes me feel worse than alone—like I'm lost and can't find my way back again.

"Jamie?" she calls from the fire.

My heart does a flop.

"Jamie?" she says again.

"Yeah." I stop, turn back. Stop again.

The wind coming down the lake is cold. I zip up my jacket. She's so blond and white in the fire's weird glow that she looks spooky.

"You shouldn't go there by yourself." Her voice flutters in the wind.

"Okay. I won't," I lie.

"I'm serious, Jamie. It's sad and scary. Not something you should do on your own."

God, I love her. She kills me.

"I'm all right. Really."

"Promise me."

"I won't be long. Are you going to be all right by yourself?"

"I'm fine," she says, and looks into the fire. "Don't worry about me."

Our old place is four cottages down the beach. Birch trees all along are lit up by the moon. Somebody's built a few steps up from the beach, but the lawn, the way it rolls upward to the cottage, has that old familiar bumpy feel. The grass needs cutting.

A flowerpot on the deck. A dead geranium. The leaves are ankle deep. Nobody's been here in quite a while.

The living room window's dark like a mouth. I think about Jonah and the whale. I stick out my hand, and it passes through air. Something's wrong. The window's gone—most of the glass, that is—and the angle of the moon, which has been rising higher and shrinking, catches big shards on a bare floor. I turn on the flashlight to see beyond the yellow leaves the wind's blown in, and there's our old brown couch. I'd forgotten about it. It looks so strange in its familiarity.

One corner of window glass remains, an ice-bright triangle. I look right behind it. Slick with moonlight and big as a fist coming at me is the piano.

My legs won't hold me up. I sit down on the deck in a pile of crinkly, cold leaves. Click off the flashlight. I feel sick. I've come all this way. I don't know what I thought I'd find, but I didn't expect this. I didn't expect that it'd still be here or that because of some weird set of circumstances, I'd actually be able to go inside. I lie back in the leaves, hug them over on top of me, and look at the moon. I wait for it to steady me.

I hear footsteps in the leaves. Maybe an animal. I lie very still.

"Jamie?"

It's Gretchen. She walks onto the deck.

I lift my head from the leaves. She lets out a scream.

"It's just me," I say, looking up at her.

She practically falls down beside me. Frantically she covers herself over in leaves, and, throwing her arm across my body, trembles up against me. I'm holding her, and she seems like a miracle.

"I love you," I say.

I didn't mean to say it right out loud.

She lifts her head. "You love me?"

"Shhhh," I say. "Lie still, okay?"

She slowly lowers her head and asks in a very careful voice, "Why are you buried in leaves?"

"I felt like it." I let my arms drop because they suddenly feel so damn heavy.

"Jamie, I love you," she says. "I loved you from the minute I first saw you standing outside Mr. Freisen's class, wearing that ugly green sweater."

"What ugly green sweater." I don't want to cry. Don't let me cry. I yawn instead and rub my eyes so she won't know.

After about a minute, she starts kissing my ear. She kisses my neck, my mouth. She's nibbling and kissing me, all soft and open, her tears all bitter and salty. She's unzipping my jacket, pulling up my shirt. Her timing is just about the worst it could possibly be. I pull her on top of me and hold her tight to make her stop. My God, all I can think about is this overwhelming fiery pain that's starting to eat up my gut.

She goes all quiet against me, so quiet you can hear the tiny rustle of leaves.

"The wind's kind of cold," I manage to say. And I finally add, whispering in her ear, "Not just yet. Okay? Gretchen?"

She rolls off me, puts her arm lightly, too carefully, across my chest. I can almost hear her thinking.

I'm shaking all over. I can't seem to stop.

"Sometimes you scare me, Jamie," she suddenly blurts out. "You scare me a lot, and that's the truth. And that's why it's really hard for me sometimes. I don't know what to do about you."

She goes quiet again, and I get this panicky feeling.

"I love you," I say. "And that scares me. Do you understand?"

"Not really," she says, her voice now muffled against my jacket.

"A lot of the time, I've got stuff going on inside my head that makes me feel like I'm living in hell. The only time it ever stops is when I'm holding you. And sometimes, even then, it doesn't go away. Then there are the times when you make me feel so peaceful that just being around you is the best thing in my whole life."

She sits straight up with her back to me. I sit up, too, and lightly brush the leaves off the back of her sweater.

She shivers. I look at the cold, high moon. A cloud drifts across it like a shadow.

"You just don't get it, do you," she says in barely a whisper. "What scares me. And what scares Scott, too. Why do you always have to dwell on suicide? On your dad's suicide? On him blowing his head off? Why can't you ever think about him when he was alive?"

"I don't know. I wish I could remember him just doing ordinary things—like sweeping the deck. Or loading up wood in the truck. Or just walking along the beach in the sunshine. But I can't."

There's a lump in my throat about the size of a granite boulder. I'm starting to feel sick. Everything seems to be spinning. I say, "I think we should go."

"Not yet," says Gretchen. "My grampa died almost two years ago. He was just about the best friend I ever had. He was the absolute best. I've never been able to talk about him without feeling totally like hell that he isn't around anymore. And here I am, finally talking about him. Can you believe this? My dad's almost never at home when you need him, so Grampa was the one, you know? He was always the one I went to whenever I felt sad or scared or just needed to talk. And I've still got his hat in my dresser, Jamie. Do you know that he used to even put aftershave on the back of his neck? Every once in a while, I'll open up the drawer and take a tiny whiff. Then I close it up fast, and I close my eyes. And there's Grampa. I swear it's true."

I don't know what to do. I don't know if I should stay or go. I don't know what to do.

Her arms come around me. That finishes me. I start to cry like a stupid little kid. I'm totally losing it. There are these awful noises, like a dying animal or something. I realize—oh, God, it's me that's making those noises. I can't stop. Gretchen keeps holding on, and holding on, and holding on, cradling my head on her shoulder.

"Be quiet, now," she whispers, "oh, be quiet, Jamie," as she strokes my back over and over again.

And then I start remembering. Everything comes in an unbelievable rush, like somebody pulled the plug out of something. I see late summer of the year my father died—the weekend before school started, the last Sunday afternoon at the cottage. Mom is packing up food in cardboard boxes. Dad's at the piano, and I'm sitting plugged into the TV. Suddenly I see him standing beside me. He leans over and carefully unplugs my headphones.

"C'mon." He straightens up. "I want to show you something."

He took me up along the road. We turned into a field and walked along the edges for quite a while, past wheat as tall as my shoulders. At the end of the field, beyond a stretch of prairie grass, a line of berry bushes appeared to fringe the crest of a hill. But when we pushed past the bushes, I discovered that what it was, really, was the rim of a very high and steep clay bank. Dad bent and picked up a rock. He threw it down toward the lake. It hurtled through the air, connected with the bank, bounced off course, connected again, flew straight into the air, and landed with a mighty splash in the water. Right then, a huge blue heron flew up from somewhere far below, its wings powerfully flapping in the air, its long spindly legs dangling under it.

We watched it soar away. Dad turned to me and said, "How did you like that surprise?"

Still startled, I said, "I liked it fine."

"Good," he said, looking back at the sky where the heron had been only seconds before. "Nature means for us to remember days like this."

It was a strange thing for him to say, since he was always so quiet and not usually given to saying much of anything. I picked up another rock and hurled it, too, though it didn't go as far as Dad's and I felt disappointed. I wanted to see another heron.

With the ghost of a smile, Dad said, "We were lucky to see just one. I didn't know if the rock would work, but there you are. Usually I sit up here for quite a while and wait, but it was almost time to leave for the city and it occurred to me that you should see it. You liked it, did you?"

"I did." I was smiling at him because he seemed to need reassurance and that made me feel really sad.

"Quite a sight, wouldn't you say?"

"Yes, Dad. Yes, it was, Dad."

I felt kind of strange and giddy, like you do on cooler days when you've had too much oxygen and sunshine. Then I went like any kid to the edge of the cliff, testing it with my foot. Shale and brown clay bounced downward to the rocks and the water far below.

He was so quick that he must have reached out and grabbed the back of my sweatshirt at the same moment that I fell. He must have anticipated it, known that it might or would happen, so that he was totally prepared for me to fall and was just as prepared to keep me from falling very far.

At any rate, one moment I was sliding quickly downward, and the next I was saved, yanked back up the cliff, dragged through a bush and back from the lip of the cliff. He let go of my sweatshirt, and grabbed me tight against him, and rocked me in his arms. I could hear his heartbeat, and I remember the smoky smell of tanned moosehide before he let go and I fell backward into the prickly yellow grass.

I lay there and looked up. He stood over me, panting hard in his beautiful beaded jacket, framed tall against the bluest of heron-blue skies. I remember thinking that this was a moment I would see in my mind forever. It was the first time, I remember now, that I had ever formed such a thought.

The mind can play tricks, show you your life in random shots like a video with a crazed monkey for a cameraman. And I guess that's why you sometimes feel confused and out of control. Things go back and forth, jerk to a stop, back up, race ahead again. There's such an insane jumble that you don't even know what you're looking for. Once in a long while, though, something accidentally gets found again, and you know it for what it is. You recognize it right away. You wonder how it could ever have been lost.

Sunday at Sidonie's ✛ ✛ ✛ ✛

NOVEMBER 1960

For Kirsten and Blaine

She's seventeen. Her eyes are as gray as the ocean off the coast of France.

I just thought of that this minute, and it sounds real dumb. But I'm obsessed with her.

She says, "Kieran, I don't know anything about physics. How the hell am I going to pass my Christmas exam? Why to God did I ever decide to take twelfth-grade physics, anyway?"

"Because you wanted to keep your options open. And you're smart."

"But I hate physics."

"So drop it."

It's Sunday again, and we're sitting as usual in Sidonie's living room, studying, while a roast beef slowly turns brown in the oven.

I'm experimenting with the idea of becoming a poet.

Or a novelist, like my favorite writer, Ernest Hemingway. She says there's no money in either. I used to think I'd be a doctor, like my mother, who is always depressed, or my father, who is still drinking himself to death in Toronto, but depression and alcohol have turned me against science.

"Medicine isn't a science—it's an art," says Sidonie, whose father is a doctor, too. "And forget about your father. Don't waste your breath thinking about him. He doesn't deserve you."

Friday nights and all of Saturday, Sidonie and I spend in the car, going places or finding the nearest bush we can park behind for a few hours.

Phil—that's her sister Bobbi's fiancé—handed me half a dozen condoms last time he and Bobbi were home for the weekend. "Here," he said, "and I'll get you more if you want, so just ask. Don't pretend it isn't happening."

"It isn't," I said, looking straight at him.

"You can't keep your hands off each other," he said, "so one of these days it will. I don't want my future sister-in-law pregnant at the tender age of seventeen."

I put those condoms away where my mother wouldn't find them, and later I thanked him. He has our best interests at heart.

Phil's just got his degree in medicine. He's working at a hospital in the city. He thought for a while about coming back out here to work, at this prairie TB sanatorium where Sidonie and I are living with our parents (her widowed father, my divorced mother) until we go to the city next fall for college. But Bobbi is still there, in college, and Phil is obsessed, like me. Actually he has three obsessions—Bobbi, playing jazz piano, and medicine. In that order. So he just decided to stay put.

Guys like Phil and me are destined to be obsessed about the women in our lives. It's a good thing we fell for the right ones.

I guess you could say that I'm a really lucky guy. This place, and this house with its smell of Sunday dinner and Sidonie's head, her curly black hair, bent frustrated as hell over her physics homework, is about as far away as you could get from my former life.

Even after a year and five months of living here, I can't totally believe that the life I'm now leading is really happening. It's still like a dream that I hope I never wake up from.

In my former life in Toronto, Before Sidonie, I used to grab a pillow over my head to drown out my mom and dad, who always fought whenever he'd been drinking, which eventually got to be a constant thing. Back then, Mom referred to him as a problem drinker. After she moved out, she started calling him an alcoholic.

I used to have elaborate daydreams about getting my mother away from him. In these dreams, I threw a cloak over her and drove her to various safe places in the car in the middle of the night. Places like the west coast— Victoria, for instance, where she'd always be warm—and later, as he became more and more scary, to places where he would never think to look for her. New Orleans. New York. A dude ranch in Texas.

But she rescued herself. This made me feel weird,

because of the surprise element. Also, I wasn't included in her plans until a couple of months after she'd moved out and was living halfway across the country.

A year ago, this coming Christmas, Mom and I were getting ready to go over to the Fallows'—which is just across the street—for Christmas dinner. Everybody else was already there—the neighbors; Sidonie's aunts Monique and Lucille, whom we'd last seen in the summer; Art Barker, who is Monique's new husband; Sidonie's dad; and of course Bobbi and Phil. I could already hear Phil at the piano, taking off with this really cool version of "Jingle Bells." There was a lot of bass and some deep hilarious bonging sounds. I quickly pulled on my coat—I could hardly wait to get over there. Mom had already wandered out onto our frozen porch. She'd sprinkled herself with Nuit de Noël perfume, there was a sprig of holly in her fur jacket—she was as happy as a little girl. That's when the phone rang. It was Dad.

When the call was over, I slammed my fist into a wall. After that I walked across the street, through the snow, and the first thing I said when I saw Sidonie was, "I want to kill him."

"Your dad."

"You guessed it."

"Wasn't exactly hard to guess." She grabbed my hand; she has an unexpectedly strong grip for such a small person. We went down to their basement.

We sat on the laundry table as the laughter and music went on upstairs and we could smell the turkey and gravy and potatoes that her auntie Monique was cooking, right over our heads.

"First he tells me he's bought me this really expensive watch for Christmas," I told her. "Then he says how he's sorry, but it won't get here for a while, and I'm thinking, Yeah, lucky if it gets here by Easter. Then he starts in about how lonely he is and about how my mother is so heartless."

Sidonie rubbed and rubbed my shoulders and just let me blow off steam. I finally turned around and noticed how beautiful she looked. She had on this green clingy dress, and there was sparkly eye shadow on her eyelids. I said, "You look as good as a Christmas present."

Right then, my eyes started to burn, and I went outside. I smoked about five cigarettes—one right after the other—and she left me alone out there, stamping my feet in the cold, fighting the hard ball that had worked its way up from my goddamn chest so that I had to loosen my tie. She left me alone because she's smarter than any girl I've ever known. She knows how complicated things can get. She understands.

Every Sunday, around noon, I go over to Sidonie's. Her dad keeps more regular hours than he used to after her mom died a couple of years ago. Unless he's on call, he spends only a few hours over at the infirmary on Sundays. That's where my mom spends almost all her time, weekends included. He tells me to just be patient with her. His exact words. After I've talked to him about her, he always finishes our conversation by kind of hug-

ging my shoulders sideways against him. And that's that
until I have another episode of the crazies. Dr. Fallows
is an amazingly patient guy.

Usually by the time I get to Sidonie's on Sundays, he's
gone. She and I have the place to ourselves. We go and
spend time on the living room sofa. Quite a long time.
Those details are nobody's business but hers and mine.
After that we have lunch (usually something cold), and
often we'll go outside and fool around in the snow for a
while before we come back in to do homework or study
for exams.

Dr. Fallows gets back home by around four-thirty,
and my mom comes over around six o'clock, and we all
have dinner together. It's about the only time all week
that Mom laughs. At first she resisted these Sunday get-
togethers. Then Dr. Fallows told her, "Sidonie likes to
cook for people, and you'd be doing me a big favor to
encourage her. She won't cook a roast for just the two
of us."

A really domestic scene, wouldn't you say? Really normal. It's the way people should live. I wonder if my
mother will ever get married again. If she ever starts to
see any man on a frequent basis, he'll have to pass by me
at the door. I've got a metal-detector mind for people
who could cause untold misery. This is my father's legacy
to me.

Sidonie has this way of looking at the world that in-
cludes skies and storms and clouds and stars. I never
noticed those things before, not really. She looks at people the same way, too, as if she's always ready to be

surprised by something—either good or bad. And whatever it is, she just takes it all in, in this steady kind of way, like a ship on the water.

Phil says that she has an adventurous mind. And he says he never knows what to expect from Bobbi, who says that love has made her bold. Her exact words. She said that the day after Phil asked her to marry him. She announced to us that her wedding dress was going to be red.

Phil sat down, laughing. Red is Bobbi's favorite color.

"Formfitting, with a slit high up one side," Bobbi said devilishly. "Very traditional."

Phil told us, "Actually, if my parents were still alive, they'd approve. In China, red is a wedding color. It's considered lucky. White is for funerals."

"Well, there you are," Bobbi said. "I'll be your very traditional bride. And shock the hell out of everyone. Love has made me bold."

"You're already pretty bold," said Phil as she went and curled up on his knee. He grinned like crazy and lightly bit the back of her neck.

Scenes like that are frequent at Sidonie's house. Even though her mom was a semi-invalid for quite a few years before she died, Sidonie says her dad loved her mom the same deep way as Phil loves Bobbi. "And the way you love me." She always says this throwing her arms around me, pressing up against me, and it makes me feel like ten men. No matter how often we play this scene, and we must have played it a thousand times, it still has the same powerful effect on me.

Once in a while, Mom goes back to Toronto to visit Dad. That's her business. I can't stop her. This month she's been there twice. She thinks she owes him something. God knows what goes on in her mind to support this thought.

She says, "He's sick, Kieran."

"So? He's been sick before."

This time it's lasted quite a while longer than usual. He isn't seeing patients. Evidently he's holed up at our old house in Rosedale, where a nurse comes to look after him every day.

He's stopped drinking.

"Oh, good for him," I said to her on Friday morning before she left to go into the city and catch a plane. "That makes him a saint, does it? That makes up for everything, I guess."

She put her hand on my arm. Mom's a short, round woman. I'm six-foot-three. "He's your father," she said in this reproachful tone.

"Oh, piss on him." I pulled violently away from her. "Why do you care what happens to him? You've got a short memory, Mother. We are talking about a man who isn't even worth—"

"Kieran, watch your language."

She always says that. Always tells me to watch my language. Is it any more foul than the way my father treated her for years? Doesn't she realize that the way she acts, rushing to his side whenever he's down and out and doesn't have the power to do anything more to her, is sickening to me?

*   *   *

"I'm not going to drop physics," Sidonie says, getting up, running off to the kitchen. "No matter what," she calls. The oven door squeaks open, and fat spits loudly from the roast.

"That's good," I say, smiling into my history notes.

She appears around the corner of the dining room, holding her hand under a glass baster. "No matter even if it is stupid and I hate it. Even if it drives me absolutely bonkers. I hate giving up on things. I can't stand it."

We've had this conversation before. Many times. And in many different situations.

"I know," I say. "C'mere, okay?"

"Can't." She smiles ravishingly. She has a fabulous mouth.

"Please?"

"Later."

The afternoon turns red. The sun disappears. Sidonie's dad comes home. Mom is still in Toronto and will be back on an early Monday morning flight, and then she'll have another two-hour drive out here from the city.

"Hello, dear. What's cooking?" is what Dr. Fallows always says to Sidonie every Sunday when he comes through the front door.

Today, though, he's come in from the outside through the kitchen. I hear him take off his overshoes and drop them on the floor. Sidonie is making dessert. She's beating something up with a spoon or a fork that clinks against the side of what sounds like a glass bowl.

"Hi, Dad," she says.

I wait to hear him say what he usually says, but nothing. The clinking stops. Then they're whispering. A little break in the routine. A little private family conversation, I guess.

I flick on the TV. There's a news item about John F. Kennedy and about how on Wednesday morning his little daughter greeted him by saying, "Good morning, Mr. President." She's a cute little girl. And I like her name— Caroline. It has a nice ring to it, like a long, shiny string of bells.

Dr. Fallows comes into the living room. I sense him before I even see him. He has Sidonie's steady-ship quality. I guess that's where she got it from. He's not enthusiastic like she is, though. He doesn't exude big feelings.

I'm half aware of him walking closer. Any minute now, he'll pick up the newspaper, shake it out, sit back in the big soft Queen Anne chair near me. I'll say, "Hi," and we'll talk a bit as he occasionally looks over yesterday's newspaper at what I'm watching on TV.

He passes the chair, sits down on the couch beside me. I pull my eyes away from the screen. He's looking right at me. Leaning, with his arm sort of on the back of the sofa, facing me. He isn't smiling. In fact, he looks as if something is serious.

Right away I'm thinking about Sidonie and me. About how we've been carrying on lately. Oh, God, has he found out?

He looks away out the window at the night shadows on the white snow, collects himself, looks back at me. There are tears in his eyes!

"Kieran," he says, "I have something to tell you that's very difficult." Hesitating, he lowers his eyes, then quickly raises them again and continues, "Your dad died. A heart attack. It happened this afternoon. About an hour ago."

"Who died?"

"Your father. I am so sorry to be the one to tell you this. Your mother called me because she didn't want you to be alone. . . ."

"My dad died."

"Yes."

"Excuse me," I say. I get up and go to the front hall. My dad died. I rummage in my coat pockets for my cigarettes. I can't find them. I can't stop my hands from trembling.

"Oh, God . . . Kieran, I'm so sorry," says Sidonie, behind me. She's reaching out her arms, crying. Her face is all contorted.

I hold up my hands. "Leave me alone," I whisper. "Just . . . leave me alone, okay?"

"Okay," she sobs. "It's okay. It's okay."

"Help me find my goddamn cigarettes, okay?" I grab her head, kiss her forehead, hug her against me.

She wraps her arms tightly around me.

"Please. Let me go for now," I say. "You'll have to let me go. I'll be okay. Really."

"All right." She lets her arms drop. "All right."

"Where are my goddamn smokes? I need a cigarette so bad."

"They're in here," Dr. Fallows says in a quiet voice

from the living room. "Come back in here, Kieran. Come back and sit down."

We go back into the living room. Dr. Fallows is holding up my pack of cigarettes. I slump back down beside him. Sidonie sits in the Queen Anne chair. I can't even get a cigarette out of the pack. Dr. Fallows has to take it from me and pull one out. He doesn't smoke himself, and he doesn't approve of smoking, but he awkwardly strikes a match and cups it with his hand under the cigarette in my mouth. I take a drag. I inhale. I put the cigarette down in the ashtray.

Dr. Fallows starts talking. He says that my father was a very sick man who couldn't help himself in a lot of the things that he did. He says that over the year and a half that he's come to know me, he's impressed with the way I handle myself and the maturity that I've attained. He says that most people in my situation can't handle the pressure and end up doing things they later regret. He says that I'm a great help and comfort to my mother and that I should be proud of that. He says I'm intelligent and sentimental and that I should never feel that that is an unmanly combination.

I have a terrible headache, and I feel like throwing up. Apart from that, I don't feel much of anything. My cigarette burns a long ash in the ashtray.

"After dinner," he says, "—if you feel like eating— you could run across to your house, pack up a few things, come back here, and stay with us. Sidonie can make up a bed for you in Bobbi's room."

"When is my mother coming home?"

"She won't be home for a while. She'll stay there to sort things out."

"When is—the funeral?"

"She'll call you. She said she'd call you later on this evening. She'll make arrangements for you to go."

"To his funeral."

"Yes."

Sometime in the middle of the night, the bedroom door opens. I've been staring at the ceiling. I didn't pull the blinds. It's windy and cold outside. The moon is bright. Big, bare tree branches scrape against the windows. I slowly turn my head, and Sidonie is standing in the doorway with her cat, Bogie, under her arm. He's a tabby Manx, the biggest cat you ever saw.

Sidonie walks across the room. Bogie's loud purr is like a motor propelling Sidonie's shiplike grace. She stops by the bed and stares down at me with huge, sad eyes. She's the smartest girl alive.

"Hi. I'm not asleep," I say.

"I know," she says. "It's too much to take in all at once."

With her free arm, she reaches down and pulls back the covers, and then she and Bogie get into bed with me.

"Your dad," I say.

"Shut up," she says, flattening Bogie between us. "We've got a chaperone."

I go back to staring at the fingering shadows on the ceiling. "I've been lying here, thinking," I say. "Or trying to. But nothing's come up, you know; I just don't know what to think about what's happened. I don't know what to say."

"You don't have to say anything," she whispers, pulling the covers around her. "It isn't until people die that you understand what you've lost."

"But I'm not sad! That's the thing of it. And I don't know if I ever will be."

She shifts her head on the pillow. "Two summers ago, when you first came here, I was in pretty bad shape. Do you remember that? It was just coming onto the anniversary of Mom's death, and if it hadn't been for you, I don't know if I ever would have made it. Period."

"Why are you telling me this?"

"Because you don't have to be so damn strong. I'll take care of you. What's the worst thing that could happen?"

"I don't know."

"What's the worst thing about him dying?"

"I don't know."

"You do, too, know. You just don't dare say it."

"I never . . ." I have to stop. I don't want to think about this.

"You never told him you loved him," Sidonie finishes for me. "That's it, isn't it?"

This hurricane gathering inside me is huge and terrifying. I turn my head and feel the familiar flutter of her breath. Nothing is changed, and everything is different. "You'll stay here, won't you?"

"Where else would I go?" she says, shifting closer.

I find her hand across Bogie's back. Our held hands are deep in his warm, soft fur. We wait for the morning.

All the Stars in the Universe ✢ ✢ ✢ ✢

JULY 1961

For Sidura

So that he'll look at me, I say, "Kieran, I'm going now."
He still doesn't look up—lying on his back, his strong
fingers folding and unfolding some dumb paper airplane
he's just made out of yesterday's comics section.

I sit down again and nibble his earlobe that has the
freckle nestled right in the middle like a tiny star. "For
now and always," I whisper. "For up and down, for sideways and inside and outside and near and far away, I love
you. Okay?"

"Okay," he says, drawing in a sigh. (His hair always
smells sweet, like fresh air and raisins.) "Okay," he repeats, sitting up. "I know that. But you can say that and
you seem to know about how that might work. That it
could work. But I don't. I just don't think anything is
forever. All I see is everything ending."

Closing his eyes, he lies back on his mother's scratchy

brown sofa. I lie on top of him. I stretch myself along his long body, and if I could climb inside him, I would. I bury my nose in his neck. It's summer again. The long, hot days, his sticky skin and his pulse beating away against my lips are as familiar to me as my own breath. How could he believe that anything so solid as we've had for two years could end?

"It could end," he says, reading my mind, "just like . . . that." His whole body moves slightly under me as he raises one listless hand and on "that" snaps his fingers.

I lift my head, then roll off him against the back of the sofa. "Do you want it to end? Is that what you're telling me?"

He gets up. The sofa cushion rises. "We're still so young, Sidonie."

I can't believe what I'm hearing. "Almost eighteen. And?"

"Don't things ever scare you?"

"Yes."

"Like what?"

"I don't know! Life! The random awful things that happen to people!"

"I need some time," he says, his voice reasonable, calm. "I'm just a little confused."

"Just a little confused?"

"Yeah. Just a little."

He looks at me evenly. No emotion. The curtains are drawn behind those gold-flecked brown eyes. He's just a little confused, but other than that, everything is fine, fine, fine.

"I have to stop seeing you," he says finally. He yanks his T-shirt off the floor, pulls it over his lightly tanned body, jams his feet into his shoes.

"For how long?" I ask him, panic rising.

"I don't know for how long. I just don't know, okay? Don't ask me so many questions!"

He leaves me lying there. In *his* house. The front door opens, clicks shut. Out on the porch, the screen door creaks open, sproings shut.

I wonder if it's possible for a person to drown in their own tears. I'm just going to lie here as they scald me and find out.

At night, across the street on top of our flat roof, all the stars seem to circle in a lazy parade. If you lie up there with someone you love and try to count them, you'll go dizzy.

At one time or another, we've all been up there. Kieran and me. My sister, Bobbi, and her fiancé, Phil. And Bobbi says she bets even Mom and Dad used to go up there.

One spring day last year, after the snow had melted, I found an oval-shaped brooch hiding off in a remote corner of our roof under some leaves. I picked it up. When I'd wiped off the crud, it shone back in all these little tiny enamel inlays of bright blue and green and violet— actually, *violets*, growing up against an azure sky. I took it down to show Dad.

He was standing in the kitchen listening to the rush of spring water in the ravine far below our house.

"It's your mother's," he said.

Mom often appears in the present tense when he talks about her.

"I found it up on the roof," I said, handing it over.

He took it, palmed it for a moment, then tucked it in his shirt pocket, next to his heart.

Across the lake, on the other side of the valley, a train echoes in a rush of clackety-clacks and a long, low whistle. Hauling cargo somewhere. And at exactly two-fifty-nine, on this breathless afternoon, I hear the rattling wheeze of Phil's car. And then his and Bobbi's voices as they get out, slamming doors, laughing. Also the rattling of paper grocery bags.

Sounds always carry in the summer. Every wind-shivering leaf, every bird call, is recorded. Every pulse of summer life is hotly insistent and close to the ear.

I get off the McMorrans' sofa. I carry my shoes over to their front hall mirror. I rub the tears off my cheeks. I look like an Italian boy since I got my hair cut. Black curly hair just kind of rising up in soft surprise away from my face. I comb it back with my fingers and stare into my own eyes. Maybe I'm in shock. My eyes are so red, Goddamn it, and I can barely move in this heat.

I open the door. Heat hits me like a wall of white. I can barely see. He's gone.

Probably to swim, at the lake.

Phil was the first person, after Mom died, to see how lonely I felt. As he was falling in love with Bobbi and I was falling in love with Kieran, part of me loved Phil more fiercely than I had ever loved anyone before. We were, and still are, kindred spirits. Now all I want to do is take him aside and slip under his arm and talk to him about this crazy, confusing summer that Kieran and I have been having.

But when I get inside our kitchen, it's Bobbi who's standing there.

"Hi," she says, with a faint smile and a slight double take. "What's wrong?"

"Nothing," I say.

And then she's wrapping me up in her soft flowery-smelling embrace. My sister, who was so abrasive and filled with guilt after Mom died. It's like the old Bobbi moved out and this genuinely mature woman has taken her place. I mean, there are still hints of the old. But she's like a parched garden after the rain. No wonder Phil's so crazy about her.

I burst into tears and start to babble. "I'm so confused—I don't know how I'm going to stand it anymore."

She doesn't say, "What about?" or "Stand what?" as she would have done two years ago. She just holds me. She rocks me. She strokes my crazy hair. I sob and hold on. Her reddish blond silky hair is golden and flamy down her back, in the kitchen, with robins chirping outside.

Later, she and Phil have a beer at the kitchen table. He reaches out his hand to me. He's Canadian-born Chinese, tall, muscular in not a showy but a compact way, and he has this expression when he's feeling sorry about something, about *you*, that instantly melts off all the prickles.

He pulls me onto his lap. I know that Bobbi's talked to him. He says, "Just ride it out, honey-babe. Things might work, right?"

"I don't know."

He feeds me some beer out of a SOUTH CAROLINA, LAND OF DREAMS mug. It's been in the family so long, no one can remember who it came from.

I take a couple of sips, then get off his knee and say to them both, "Maybe it's just too intense for him. He's always saying how nothing is forever. It's become one of his favorite sayings. Nothing is forever. . . ." I stop as a fresh flow of tears runs down my face.

"He loves you, right?" Phil says.

"It's more complicated than that."

"You love him," says Bobbi, "but sometimes, for you, too, isn't it all too much?"

"No. And now I'm going to be so lonely."

Bobbi looks across at Phil. He's developed this habit of staring back at her even when he's so uncomfortable that even I can't watch. It's as if he made up his mind when his parents died that he would try very hard not to close his eyes on the people who are still alive. For fear of missing something.

"Sidonie," says Bobbi, "let some time pass. It won't kill either one of you. Get some breathing space."

"Then you'll know," says Phil.

"*I'll* know?"

"You both will know," says Bobbi.

When the world cooled down, and after Dad came home; after hot dogs on the barbecue; after Phil pushing Bobbi on the swing in the front garden so that her toes seemed to touch the treetops on the other side of the ravine; after the sun retreated and the moon, a dazed adventurer behind a mist of mauve cloud, rose up and hung over the lake; after Donina Stang's one-year-old black Lab barked in their front yard for her and her husband, Gerry, to hurry after him down to the water for a moonlight dip; after the velvet black of eleven-thirty at night; after that, the stars above the roof of our square flattop house revolved in space.

I took my sleeping bag up to the roof and crawled inside and looked up. The sky was never more beautiful—like a cathedral. And I slept.

In the morning, I decided a mattress would make a good addition to my open-air bedroom. That and some mosquito netting.

The morning after that, I watched the top of Dad's head, the bald spot clearly visible as he left the house and ambled down the sidewalk.

"Hi," I said.

He looked up. "My God!"

I lifted my arms. "I'm an eagle."

"What are you doing up there in your pajamas?"

"This is my new bedroom."

"I think Bobbi and Phil are getting ready to go back to the city." He paused. "Are you coming down soon?"

"Yes."

"I made French toast. I left some in the oven. There's a bowl of strawberries on the counter."

"I'm fine. Don't worry about me."

"I'll be home early."

"You don't have to come home early."

"Just the same. Do you want to go to Crystal Lake and a movie later on tonight? We could stop and get a bucket of chicken."

"No, Dad. I just want to be by myself."

"Maybe you two were spending too much time together."

"Dad!"

"I'll see you later."

The weekend was over. Then another week. And another weekend. I got a letter from Winnipeg telling me that I'd been accepted into the University of Manitoba. I wondered if Kieran had gotten his letter yet. I saw him all the time, walking down to the beach in his dark blue bathing suit, his summer tan getting darker each day. I saw him and his mom, Dr. McMorran, drive off for groceries to Crystal Lake, fifteen miles down the valley. I saw him cut Donina Stang's lawn and paint dark green trim on Mr. and Mrs. Coates's house.

I thought about the first time I saw him, three summers before, the new boy from Ontario who seemed to have a blueprint on sophistication while I was still wearing my funny tartan bathing suit that I'd gotten when I was twelve years old. I thought about his now dead father, who had never touched him but had left his mother scarred in places that clothing usually covers. And I thought about the bank account this man left to his son—thousands and thousands of dollars to pay for an education.

"Blood money. I'll never give that bastard the satisfaction," Kieran said the day he came home from his father's funeral. "I'll never be what he wanted me to be—a doctor, like him. Divine healer with blood on his hands."

I remember thinking that the anger would gradually go away. That he'd forget and his mother would forget. Because time, I've discovered, does take care of a lot of things.

Mid-July, and I've taken to lighting candles high up in my eagle's nest.

I am fine. I'm not as lonely as I thought I would be. My father sleeps far below in his bedroom, dreaming, maybe, of my mother as the stars slowly revolve in space.

It is midnight, and I'm sitting straight up and I'm contemplating a sky full of stars.

One of the stars is not a star at all. It's a firefly. I watch it zigzag up over our roof and trail its little light down toward the street. I stand up with my candle and walk over to where the tops of trees greet me in total silence. It's such a still night.

Across the way, just above the McMorrans' roof, which is slanted, not flat like ours, I see another firefly. It dances on the edge, then disappears. Half a second later, right where it was, a thin candle flame flickers upward, and in the darkness, I can just begin to make out a human form outlined against a backdrop of sky.

He's over there. On that dangerous roof. With a lighted candle. He starts to whistle. He's doing his Maurice Chevalier impression. He doesn't have to sing the words—I can hear them in his florid tones. "Everrry leeetle brrrreeeeze seems to wheesperrr Lou-ise."

How long has he been sitting there? I call across to him, "What are you doing?"

He stops in mid-warble. "I'm sitting in the dark with a candle."

"I can see that. *Why?*"

"I'm trying to attract attention."

"Oh, very good. I'm so impressed."

"It's dangerous," he calls over. "I like that. The danger."

"Big deal."

"Can I come over?"

"No."

"Why not?"

"Because. I'm not talking to you."

"You just did."

"Take a flying leap, McMorran."

"I might just do that," he says with a cackle.

I walk away. I sit down on my sleeping bag and try to concentrate on the stars. But I can still hear him cackling over there, and I want to smack him for disturbing all my hard-earned peace.

The next night, I'm lying flat on my back on this speck of a planet. I am thinking about the immensity of the Milky Way. I'm thinking about how in Africa, at this very moment, somebody could be looking up at the universe and thinking the very same thought.

The square box that fits down over the stairs leading to the rooftop lifts up, slowly scratches across the heavy tar-paper roofing, then slumps down in the darkness. I continue my contemplation of the stars.

Someone is standing over me. I know, without looking, who it is.

"Hi," he says.

I do not respond. I will him to go away. I do not want to feel the things he makes me feel. I want the peace of the stars. I want the dark, quiet night with the trains running in the distance.

"Are you still talking to me?" he says, hunkering down.

"No."

"Why not?"

"Go away."

"That's not an answer," he says. "Can't we be friends for at least five minutes?"

"Why?"

"Please?" He slips off his shoes. Pauses. Then he cautiously unzips the sleeping bag and slips in beside me. With slow deliberation, he turns sideways, facing my ear. He barely brushes my hair with his lips. "I'm sorry for hurting you," he whispers.

"You broke my heart."

"I never meant to."

"But you did, anyway. And I'm not going to put up with it."

"You always were a fighter, Sidonie. You're formidable

when you don't get the things you want. I was beginning to wonder if I had the strength to fight for anything at all. Without you. And that scared me."

"You didn't have to leave me."

"Yes, I did. Sometimes I don't know where you begin and I leave off. Until I met you, I had a shitty life, and a lot of it wasn't my fault. It just happened."

I think about what I told him when we broke up, about the random awful things that happen to people in this world. But up there—up above—is this perfect sense of order.

I sink down until just the top of my head and my eyes stick out of the sleeping bag. I look for the star that has my mother's name on it. It's the one that rises closest to the moon. It's quite big. I don't suppose it's a star at all. It's probably a planet.

"Nothing is forever," I tell him. "You were right all along."

Kieran rolls over onto his back. "I thought about my dad quite a bit while I was away from you, going crazy all by myself for a change. It was actually good to think about him. Even if he wasn't the best person in the world, he had his moments. I remember, when I was around eleven or twelve, him taking me midnight fishing. We stood on the dock. Under the full moon. And that night the lake seemed as big as the universe. We didn't catch anything, but that wasn't what was important. What was, what really mattered, was us. And the way those silvery lines went whishing away. The way they both went, sometimes together and sometimes apart, out into that big, black scary lake."

We shiver in the darkness. Kieran slips his arm under me and pulls me close. We hang on to each other and watch the ghostly stars revolve in space.

A Wedding ┼ ┼ ┼ ┼

AUGUST 1962

Sometimes, when Bobbi and I get together and she takes in a deep, quick breath of contentment or laughs uncontrollably at things that only she and I find funny, I see a piece of Mom. It's the sort of thing that catches my heart and makes me ache to see her again—all of her, not just a fragment. Even if only a ghost.

Last night, the skin under her eyes gray with pre-wedding fatigue, Bobbi said, "There are no roses in this house. So why do I keep smelling them?"

I was sitting on the bathroom floor and I looked up, startled by what she'd said, accidentally smudging the shell-pink polish on my big toe.

"Sidonie," she said, "what do you think?"

I eased the nail polish brush back into its pot. "I think," I said, "that I'm glad I'm not going crazy. I'm glad somebody is finally saying it out loud."

She sank deeper into the tub, her skin squeaking along the bottom. "So you smell them, too."

"The windows are always open," I offered.

"So you think it's coming from her rose garden." She hung a steamy washcloth over her face and breathed deeply.

"Can you still smell it?"

"No," she replied in a small, muffled voice.

"You're lying through your teeth."

"Oh, God," said Bobbi, her voice suddenly breaking, "I still miss her so much."

I got up and went over and pulled the cloth off her face and kissed her on both cheeks, the French way, the way Mom would have done. Bobbi and I have discovered over the past four years, since Mom's death, that we both cry at the weirdest times. This spring, for instance, when Bobbi was on her way to take an anatomy exam, a woman got on the bus wearing a blue hat. It triggered a whole bunch of memories. Bobbi burst into tears on the bus, and then she cried all through her exam. She felt like an idiot.

Anyway, last night, the night before her wedding, as I held her in my arms and got sopping wet and smelled the clean soap smell on her skin, that other smell, the roses smell, seemed to disappear. Did it just gather together in a little invisible cloud and seep away under the bathroom door?

Today, in Dad's bedroom, I'm helping Kieran with his tie. He looks over my shoulder at his reflection in Mom's old full-length mirror. The afternoon sun, streaming through the window, gives his dark suit a kind of dazzling glow.

There's a moment of dizzying blindness. And just before my vision clears, I hear the swish of Mom's skirts moving across the carpet behind me.

But there is a rational explanation for this. Here we are replaying a familiar scene: Mom and Dad getting ready for a special occasion. Brushing across my memory is him fastening the small black hook at the back of her taffeta evening dress. She turns, lifting a perfumed hand, and folds his suit collar into place. A glance, which excludes Bobbi and me, passes between them.

"Hot damn," Kieran says, leaning a little to the left, "I look good."

"Where is he?" I mutter. "You'd think he could at least be on time for his own daughter's wedding."

"Sidonie, for the tenth time, stop worrying." Lowering his head, he nibbles my lips with a kiss. He pulls me against him. "And what are you doing later, young lady? How about the rooftop at around nine?"

I look up at him. He is so chipper. So proud that Phil has chosen him to be his best man.

Kieran suddenly frowns. I realize I'm crying.

"I'm sorry for being such a sap," I blubber.

"Your mom, right? Look, you don't have to apologize." He pulls the white handkerchief from his breast pocket and awkwardly dabs at my tears. Mascara comes off on his handkerchief. "Everything's going to be fine," he says. "It'll be a great wedding. And I know you'll miss her. But that's just the way it goes, right?"

He's stated the simple truth. But it hits a nerve.

I take the handkerchief from him, shove it back in his pocket, and say, "She would have loved Bobbi's wedding. It's not fair that she isn't here."

Bobbi is having her own nervous breakdown. Fifteen minutes ago, as we finished getting dressed, she burst into tears because she couldn't find the chain with the gold cross that Mom gave her. She wanted to wear it for something old.

We pulled out all her drawers. We emptied all her little jewelry boxes.

"Bobbi," I finally said, "you'll be fine without it. You won't need it. Really."

"But what if I've lost it?"

It was at that point that Bobbi became totally inconsolable.

"Do you want me to leave you alone for a while?"

She nodded. I replaced the bobby pin that was falling out of her French roll and left her.

Maybe she and Phil shouldn't have chosen a date so close to the anniversary of Mom's death. But Mom actually died on my birthday, and that wasn't exactly what you'd call impeccable timing, either.

And now Phil is gently knuckling his way into her room.

"Bobbi," he whispers hoarsely, "are you going to be all right? Let me in. Please."

He opens Bobbi's bedroom door a few inches. A smooth hand, glittering with the diamond he gave her two Christmases ago, appears almost by itself—seemingly unattached to a body. The hand grips Phil's. He is pulled into the bedroom, and the door quickly shuts behind him.

"If this wedding gets off the ground, it'll be a miracle," I say to Kieran in the upstairs hallway. "And I'm *so* mad at Dad. Why couldn't he find somebody else to look after his patients? This is a once-in-a-lifetime day. I want to strangle him."

Kieran laces his fingers with mine. "He's given up a lot of time lately, to help organize it all."

"You're always sticking up for him. He doesn't need your help, you know."

"Of course he does. Trapped in a household with two bossy women."

Halfway down the stairs, we reach the second landing. A small window at floor level looks out to the tall green oak trees. The front door opens, bangs shut. Dad dashes around the hall corner, harried, sweaty, and bounds up the stairs toward us, loose change jingling in his pocket.

"Who spilled the perfume?" he asks, reaching the landing.

"What perfume?" I ask, startled.

"Your mother never wore perfume," he pronounces in a rather grumpy way, and he leaps on past.

I am indignant. I run up after him. "She did so wear perfume! How could you have forgotten that! She wore Chanel Number Five! Just a little dabbed behind each ear!"

"You look beautiful, anyway. And that's a very becoming shade of green," he says sheepishly, just before his bedroom door closes.

He turns on the transistor radio that he keeps on top of his dresser beside Mom's picture. Immediately there's Hank Williams singing "There's a Bluebird on Your Windowsill." It's a song that Mom used to whistle around the house. It's not the only song, of course. But I don't want to hear any of them on Bobbi's wedding day.

I go back and sink down on the landing. Kieran eases down alongside me. He stares helplessly at his feet.

"Just hold me, okay?" I say miserably, leaning against him.

He draws in a breath and reaches an arm around me. "You're a mess," he says, nuzzling his chin on the top of my head. "You're going to have to pull yourself together."

"I know it," I sniff. "I know that."

Auntie Monique appears below us in the front hall.

"Come here, *petit chou*," she clucks.

She's wearing a dark pink satin sheath, a frilly white apron tied around her plump middle.

"Now, now," she says. "That sister of yours is just crying tears of joy up there, and you mustn't worry about it."

"I'm not."

I pull Kieran after me down the stairs.

"Next thing—you two, eh?" She laughs as we reach her and pinches my chin. "I was just saying to your auntie Lucille and my Art Barker at breakfast this morning, that Sidonie and Kieran—oh, my!"

Clasping her hand over her heart, she lets out another of her laughs that always make me think of Mom.

Kieran dazzles her with a smile, then leans over and lightly grazes her cheek with a kiss.

"I'll go check on the champagne," she says, quickly dabbing her eyes. "A wedding in this house. Your mama would be so pleased." She drops her hand. "Now, look at that old cat. He still has so much life!"

Bogie comes charging out of the living room into the hall, his toes scratching frantically over the hardwood. We asked the florist at Crystal Lake to make him a collar out of blue ribbon, with a flower and some fern. He's somehow managed to yank the whole thing off and is punting it around the floor. It looks like hell.

Suddenly he stops and starts to gag.

"Bogie! Don't throw up, don't throw up!" I scoop him into my arms and dash him outside. He kecks up an immense fur ball, mixed with petals and greenery and bits of ribbon, on the front step.

Kieran hoses down the steps just as the guests start to arrive: Irvine and Walda Genaske—friends of Bobbi and Phil from the city—and their two little daughters. Then along comes the sanatorium superintendent, Dr. Jennings, and his wife, Margaret, and one of Bobbi's profs, Dr. Gladys Lindstrom. The neighbors, Donina and Gerry Stang, and Mr. and Mrs. Coates, walk over together from their houses across the street, followed shortly after that by Kieran's mom.

"Isn't your brother, George, here today?" Dr. Jennings asks Phil in the living room.

"He's on sabbatical for a year. In England." Phil nervously looks over a glass of pink punch toward the stairs. She's still up there.

"Ah." Dr. Jennings sips his own punch. "I enjoyed meeting him last summer. And his beautiful wife . . ." He pauses, searching his memory.

"Lila," Phil finishes for him.

"Yes. Lila. What a *celestial* name."

"Yes," says Phil. "Excuse me, please, Dr. Jennings."

Phil walks into the sunny dining room, taking Kieran with him. They stand in private conversation, these two men I love. Stand by the table, made long for the occasion, that I covered with the snowiest of white linen. A flash of memory, and Mom's hand glides an iron carefully over its surface. I breathe in, then out. I go up the stairs.

The door to Bobbi's bedroom is slightly ajar. I hear Dad's low voice as the door swishes across the carpet and I walk in.

Bobbi's slim wedding dress is a long red Chinese brocade, and her strawberry blond hair is pulled back with a circlet of baby's breath. Her face is still a bit blotchy, but her big green eyes are clear.

Dad, finally dressed, sits beside her on the edge of the bed.

Slowly twirling a white rose, his boutonniere, in one hand, he glances up and says, "Your sister misses your mother. She wishes she were here today."

I lift the chair from under Bobbi's vanity and set it down beside the bed.

"I want to tell you something," I say to him.

"Oh?" He raises his head.

"It concerns a certain scent. Maybe what you thought was perfume. But maybe it wasn't."

"Oh, that," says Bobbi, embarrassed. "That isn't anything, I'm sure. Just us going crazy. Or something."

Dad listens, methodically rubbing a shiny black shoe over the nap of the bedroom carpet, as I tell him about the scent of the roses. When I'm finished, he nods, a few times, stands up, and looks out Bobbi's window.

"After your mother died," he says, "on the morning after, I woke up hearing music. The most beautiful music I'd ever heard." He turns around to look at us. "It didn't mean that she was there. Or anything like that. I think I was having what's called an auditory hallucination. I couldn't believe she was gone, you see."

He stops, stricken afresh by this memory, and seems unable to continue.

Bobbi's perched on the edge of the bed, feet pigeon-toed, lashes blinking, caught by his wonder and his sorrow, by the love he still feels for our mother.

I get up and take Dad's warm hand, swinging it back and forth to comfort him because that's all I can think of to do.

"I'm fine," he says, smiling at me.

"I know." I smile back. "We're all fine."

I look swiftly over at Bobbi. She is smiling at her hands. They have floated up from her knees.

Here is the moment before a new life starts. Here is the family snapshot that nobody takes. This one is portable. This one travels light.

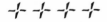

Martha Brooks is an award-winning novelist, playwright, and writer of short fiction. For the past ten years she has taught creative writing to high school students, the very people who inspire her writing. In speaking about *Traveling On into the Light*, she says, "This book is about the power of memory, loss, isolation, love, and unexpected connections. Each story is a window on the lives of young people who are trying to reach the light. Each finds their lighted path through various means: the kindness of strangers; the powerful support of friends, family, or lovers; the sanctity of a safe place from which personal dragons can finally be faced." In a starred review *School Library Journal* called her first collection of short stories, *Paradise Café and Other Stories*, "tiny masterpieces. . . . [H]er style sings." It was chosen a *School Library Journal* Best Book of the Year and was a Boston Globe–Horn Book Honor Book for Fiction in 1991. Her novel, *Two Moons in August*, was chosen a Best Book for Young Adults by the American Library Association and was nominated for the Governor General's Award for Children's Literature in Canada. Martha Brooks lives in Winnipeg, Manitoba, Canada, with her husband and daughter.

-┼- -┼- -┼- -┼-